Praise for *The Color Purple*

'The great irony about *The Color Purple* is that it transcends colour. To do that you have to be a magician or a genius. This book works on all levels, the political, the historical, the personal, the emotional, the spiritual . . . If you are not touched by this book you can't be touched. Not a word is wasted, every breath is accounted for. We all know that this is one of the greatest books of all time. It's a no brainer'

Benjamin Zephaniah

'I got the book and read it, in one day, when it came out. And then I went back, the next day, and bought every copy they had'

Oprah Winfrey

'Pathbreaking in its willingness to scrutinise violence and pathologies within the family and inside beleaguered communities, *The Color Purple* helped embolden many others to follow. Yet it did so with a wit and warmth, and a faith in redemptive love and transformative art, that are Walker's own. It can be difficult, 25 years on, to grasp the strength of the taboos that she, and a few peers, were assailing. But that they no longer have the power to silence owes something to this work'

Maya Jaggi

'*The Color Purple* is my go-to comfort novel. Every single time I read this book, I walk away as a slightly better person than I was when I picked it up'

Tayari Jones

'I think that *The Color Purple* was the first book that made me think that I could try to be a writer – or that made me aware that a young Black woman from the South could write about the South'

Jesmyn Ward

'*The Color Purple* is a lush celebration of all that it means to be female, to be a Black female and like the best of celebrations, it is an honest one. Alice Walker's honesty in this book is combative, relentless and redemptive. It is from this honesty that bitterness emerges, and yet the bitterness never blights the encompassing humanity of Walker's vision. I love that *The Color Purple* doesn't try to soften its blows but is also courageous enough to hold on to a wonderfully affirming faith in possibility, in forgiveness and kindness and hope. I love the urgency of Walker's language, the bite of her humor, her continual engagement with the spiritual and the sexual, her portraits of female friendships, and her ambitious reaching across of the Africa-Black America divide'   Chimamanda Ngozi Adichie

'*The Color Purple* was what church should have been, what honest familial reckoning could have been, and it is still the only art object in the world by which all three generations of Black artists in my family judge American art'   Kiese Laymon

'*The Color Purple* is a story that stays with you forever. It's there morning, noon and night and right beside you every time you try and lose yourself in another tale. It's been with me for twenty years now and refuses to gather dust on the bookshelf of my life'   Dotun Adebayo

'I was afraid and insecure when I read this book. Families are not always sanctuaries. This book and a couple of others came at the right time to make me see it was possible to be strong and not choked up with self pity'   Yasmin Alibhai-Brown

'I associate closely with Alice Walker's novels – you can't divorce yourself from hope, otherwise there's nothing left'   Corinne Bailey Rae

'One of the most haunting books you could ever wish to read . . . it is stunning – moving, exciting, and wonderful'
                                                                    Lenny Henry

'One of the most gifted writers in her country'   Isabel Allende

'A unique blend of serenity and immediacy that makes your senses ache'   Helen Dunmore

'One of those few writers of fiction concerning whom comparisons are immaterial. She is truly herself, and a truly wonderful writer'   Allan Massie

'*The Color Purple* is a work to stand beside literature for any time and any place. It needs no other category other than the fact that it is superb'   Rita Mae Brown

'Alice Walker is a lavishly gifted writer'   *New York Times*

'A fable for the modern world'   *Washington Post*

'Places Walker in the company of Faulkner'   *The Nation*

'Intense emotional impact . . . Indelibly affecting . . . Alice Walker is a lavishly gifted writer'
                                            New York Times Book Review

'*The Color Purple* is an American novel of permanent importance'   *Newsweek*

'Superb . . . A work to stand beside literature of any time and place'   *San Francisco Chronicle*

'A lovely, painful book. Walker's finest novel'   *Kirkus*

'A magical and moving climax enhanced by Walker's exceptionally eloquent prose'   *Booklist*

'A stunning, brilliantly conceived book . . . a saga filled with joy and pain, humor and bitterness, and an array of characters who live, breathe and illuminate the world of Black women'
Publishers Weekly

'Trying to synopsize this beautiful novel is like trying to summarize the Bayeux tapestry . . . It is disturbing, and it is exhilarating'   *New York Daily News*

'Marvelous characters . . . A story of revelation . . . One of the great books of our time'   *Essence*

ALICE WALKER, winner of the Pulitzer Prize and the National Book Award, is a canonical figure in American letters. She is the author of *The Color Purple*, *The Temple of My Familiar*, *Horses Make a Landscape Look More Beautiful*, *The Way Forward Is with a Broken Heart*, *Now Is the Time to Open Your Heart* and many other works of fiction, poetry, and nonfiction. Her writings have been translated into more than two dozen languages, and more than fifteen million copies of her books have been sold worldwide.

ALSO BY ALICE WALKER

Fiction

The Third Life of Grange Copeland

*In Love & Trouble:
Stories of Black Women*

Meridian

*You Can't Keep a Good
Woman Down: Stories*

To Hell With Dying

The Temple of My Familiar

Finding the Green Stone

Possessing the Secret of Joy

The Complete Stories

By the Light of My Father's Smile

The Way Forward Is with a Broken Heart

Now Is the Time to Open Your Heart

Poetry

Once

Revolutionary Petunias and Other Poems

*Good Night, Willie Lee, I'll
See You in the Morning*

*Horses Make a Landscape
Look More Beautiful*

*Her Blue Body Everything We
Know: Earthling Poems*

*Absolute Trust in the Goodness
of the Earth*

*A Poem Traveled Down My
Arm: Poems and Drawings*

Collected Poems

*Hard Times Require Furious
Dancing: New Poems*

Taking the Arrow Out of the Heart

Nonfiction

*In Search of Our Mothers'
Gardens: Womanist Prose*

Living by the Word

Warrior Marks

*The Same River Twice:
Honoring the Difficult*

*Anything We Love Can Be
Saved: A Writer's Activism*

*Pema Chödrön and Alice
Walker in Conversation*

*Sent by Earth: A Message from
the Grandmother Spirit*

*We Are the Ones We Have Been
Waiting For*

Overcoming Speechlessness

The Chicken Chronicles: A Memoir

*The Cushion in the Road: Meditation
and Wandering as the Whole World
Awakens to Be in Harm's Way*

*Gathering Blossoms Under Fire: The
Journals of Alice Walker* (edited by
Valerie Boyd)

The Color Purple by Alice Walker

40th Anniversary Special Edition

WEIDENFELD & NICOLSON

First published in Great Britain in 1983
by The Women's Press
This edition first published in 2022
by Weidenfeld & Nicolson
an imprint of the Orion Publishing Group Ltd,
Carmelite House, 50 Victoria Embankment,
London EC4Y 0DZ

An Hachette UK company

First published in the United States of America in 1983
by Harcourt Brace Jovanovich, Inc.

5 7 9 10 8 6

A CIP catalogue record for this book
is available from the British Library.

ISBN (40th Anniversary Edition Hardback) 978 1 4746 2558 6
ISBN (eBook) 978 1 4091 3926 3

Typeset by Input Data Services Ltd, Somerset

Printed and bound in Great Britain by Clays Ltd, Elcograf S.p.A.

MIX
Paper from
responsible sources
FSC® C104740

www.weidenfeldandnicolson.co.uk
www.orionbooks.co.uk

To the Spirit:

Without whose assistance
Neither this book
Nor I
Would have been
Written

Show me how to do it like you
Show me how to do it.
— Stevie Wonder

The
Color
Purple

You better not never tell nobody but God. It'd kill your mammy.

Dear God,

I am fourteen years old. ~~I am~~ I have always been a good girl. Maybe you can give me a sign letting me know what is happening to me.

Last spring after little Lucious come I heard them fussing. He was pulling on her arm. She say It too soon, Fonso, I ain't well. Finally he leave her alone. A week go by, he pulling on her arm again. She say Naw, I ain't gonna. Can't you see I'm already half dead, an all of these chilren.

She went to visit her sister doctor over Macon. Left me to see after the others. He never had a kine word to say to me. Just say You gonna do what your mammy wouldn't. First he put his thing up gainst my hip and sort of wiggle it around. Then he grab hold my titties. Then he push his thing inside my pussy. When that hurt, I cry. He start to choke me, saying You better shut up and git used to it.

But I don't never git used to it. And now I feels sick every time I be the one to cook. My mama she fuss at me an look at me. She happy, cause he good to her now. But too sick to last long.

Dear God,

My mama dead. She die screaming and cussing. She scream at me. She cuss at me. I'm big. I can't move fast enough. By time I git back from the well, the water be warm. By time I git the tray ready the food be cold. By time I git all the children ready for school it be dinner time. He don't say nothing. He set there by the bed holding her hand an cryin, talking bout don't leave me, don't go.

She ast me bout the first one Whose it is? I say God's. I don't know no other man or what else to say. When I start to hurt and then my stomach start moving and then that little baby come out my pussy chewing on it fist you could have knock me over with a feather.

Don't nobody come see us.

She got sicker an sicker.

Finally she ast Where it is?

I say God took it.

He took it. He took it while I was sleeping. Kilt it out there in the woods. Kill this one too, if he can.

Dear God,

He act like he can't stand me no more. Say I'm evil an always up to no good. He took my other little baby, a boy this time. But I don't think he kilt it. I think he sold it to a man an his wife over Monticello. I got breasts full of milk running down myself. He say Why don't you look decent? Put on something. But what I'm sposed to put on? I don't have nothing.

I keep hoping he fine somebody to marry. I see him looking at my little sister. She scared. But I say I'll take care of you. With God help.

Dear God,

He come home with a girl from round Gray. She be my age but they married. He be on her all the time. She walk round like she don't know what hit her. I think she thought she love him. But he got so many of us. All needing somethin.

My little sister Nettie is got a boyfriend in the same shape almost as Pa. His wife died. She was kilt by her boyfriend coming home from church. He got only three children though. He seen Nettie in church and now every Sunday evening here come Mr ———. I tell Nettie to keep at her books. It be more then a notion taking care of children ain't even yourn. And look what happen to Ma.

Dear God,

He beat me today cause he say I winked at a boy in church. I may have got somethin in my eye but I didn't wink. I don't even look at mens. That's the truth. I look at women, tho, cause I'm not scared of them. Maybe cause my mama cuss me you think I kept mad at her. But I ain't. I felt sorry for mama. Trying to believe his story kilt her.

Sometime he still be looking at Nettie, but I always git in his light. Now I tell her to marry Mr ———. I don't tell her why.

I say Marry him, Nettie, an try to have one good year out your life. After that, I know she be big.

But me, never again. A girl at church say you git big if you bleed every month. I don't bleed no more.

Dear God,

Mr —— finally come right out an ast for Nettie hand in marriage. But He won't let her go. He say she too young, no experience. Say Mr —— got too many children already. Plus What about the scandal his wife cause when somebody kill her? And what about all this stuff he hear bout Shug Avery? What bout that?

I ast our new mammy bout Shug Avery. What it is? I ast. She don't know but she say she gon fine out.

She do more then that. She git a picture. The first one of a real person I ever seen. She say Mr —— was taking somethin out his billfold to show Pa an it fell out an slid under the table. Shug Avery was a woman. The most beautiful woman I ever saw. She more pretty then my mama. She bout ten thousand times more prettier then me. I see her there in furs. Her face rouge. Her hair like somethin tail. She grinning with her foot up on somebody motocar. Her eyes serious tho. Sad some.

I ast her to give me the picture. An all night long I stare at it. An now when I dream, I dream of Shug Avery. She be dress to kill, whirling an laughing.

Dear God,

I ast him to take me instead of Nettie while our new mammy sick. But he just ast me what I'm talking bout. I tell him I can fix myself up for him. I duck into my room and come out wearing horsehair, feathers, and a pair of our new mammy high heel shoes. He beat me for dressing trampy but he do it to me anyway.

Mr —— come that evening. I'm in the bed crying. Nettie she finally see the light of day, clear. Our new mammy she see it too. She in her room crying. Nettie tend to first one, then the other. She so scared she go out doors and vomit. But not out front where the two mens is.

Mr —— say, Well Sir, I sure hope you done change your mind.

He say, Naw, Can't say I is.

Mr —— say, Well, you know, my poor little ones sure could use a mother.

Well, He say, real slow, I can't let you have Nettie. She too young. Don't know nothing but what you tell her. Sides, I want her to git some more schooling. Make a schoolteacher out of her. But I can let you have Celie. She the oldest anyway. She ought to marry first. She ain't fresh tho, but I specs you know that. She spoiled. Twice. But you don't need a fresh woman no how. I got a fresh one in there myself and she sick all the time. He spit, over the railing. The children git on her nerve, she not much of a cook. And she big already.

Mr —— he don't say nothing. I stop crying I'm so surprise.

She ugly. He say. But she ain't no stranger to hard work. And she clean. And God done fixed her. You can do everything just like you want to and she ain't gonna make you feed it or clothe it.

Mr —— still don't say nothing. I take out the picture of Shug Avery. I look into her eyes. Her eyes say Yeah, it *bees* that way sometime.

Fact is, he say, I got to git rid of her. She too old to be living here at home. And she a bad influence on my other girls. She'd come with her own linen. She can take that cow she raise down there back of the crib. But Nettie you flat out can't have. Not now. Not never.

Mr —— finally speak. Clearing his throat. I ain't never really look at that one, he say.

Well, next time you come you can look at her. She ugly. Don't even look like she kin to Nettie. But she'll make the better wife. She ain't smart either, and I'll just be fair, you have to watch her or she'll give away everything you own. But she can work like a man.

Mr —— say How old she is?

He say, She near twenty. And another thing – She tell lies.

Dear God,

It took him the whole spring, from March to June, to make up his mind to take me. All I thought about was Nettie. How she could come to me if I marry him and he be so love struck with her I could figure out a way for us to run away. Us both be hitting Nettie's schoolbooks pretty hard, cause us know we got to be smart to git away. I know I'm not as pretty or as smart as Nettie, but *she* say I ain't dumb.

The way you know who discover America, Nettie say, is think bout cucumbers. That what Columbus sound like. I learned all about Columbus in first grade, but look like he the first thing I forgot. She say Columbus come here in boats call the Neater, the Peter, and the Santomareater. Indians so nice to him he force a bunch of 'em back home with him to wait on the queen.

But it hard to think with gitting married to Mr —— hanging over my head.

The first time I got big Pa took me out of school. He never care that I love it. Nettie stood there at the gate holding tight to my hand. I was all dress for first day. You too dumb to keep going to school, Pa say. Nettie the clever one in this bunch.

But Pa, Nettie say, crying, Celie smart too. Even Miss Beasley say so. Nettie dote on Miss Beasley. Think nobody like her in the world.

Pa say, Whoever listen to anything Addie Beasley have to say. She run off at the mouth so much no man would have her. That how come she have to teach school. He never look up from cleaning his gun. Pretty soon a bunch of white mens come walking cross the yard. They have guns too.

Pa git up and follow 'em. The rest of the week I vomit and dress wild game.

But Nettie never give up. Next think I know Miss Beasley at our house trying to talk to Pa. She say long as she been a teacher she never know nobody want to learn bad as Nettie and me. But when Pa call me out and she see how tight my dress is, she stop talking and go.

Nettie still don't understand. I don't neither. All us notice is I'm all the time sick and fat.

I feel bad sometime Nettie done pass me in learnin. But look like nothing she say can git in my brain and stay. She try to tell me something bout the ground not being flat. I just say, Yeah, like I know it. I never tell her how flat it look to me.

Mr —— come finally one day looking all drug out. The woman he had helping him done quit. His mammy done said No More.

He say, Let me see her again.

Pa call me. *Celie*, he say. Like it wasn't nothing. Mr —— want another look at you.

I go stand in the door. The sun shine in my eyes. He's still up on his horse. He look me up and down.

Pa rattle his newspaper. Move up, he won't bite, he say.

I go closer to the steps, but not too close cause I'm a little scared of his horse.

Turn round, Pa say.

I turn round. One of my little brothers come up. I think it was Lucious. He fat and playful, all the time munching on something.

He say, What you doing that for?

Pa say, Your sister thinking bout marriage.

Didn't mean nothing to him. He pull my dresstail and ast can he have some blackberry jam out the safe.

I say, Yeah.

She good with children, Pa say, rattling his paper open more. Never heard her say a hard word to nary one of them. Just give 'em everything they ast for, is the only problem.

Mr —— say, That cow still coming?

He say, Her cow.

Dear God,

I spend my wedding day running from the oldest boy. He twelve. His mama died in his arms and he don't want to hear nothing bout no new one. He pick up a rock and laid my head open. The blood run all down tween my breasts. His daddy say Don't *do* that! But that's all he say. He got four children, instead of three, two boys and two girls. The girls hair ain't been comb since their mammy died. I tell him I'll just have to shave it off. Start fresh. He say bad luck to cut a woman hair. So after I bandage my head best I can and cook dinner – they have a spring, not a well, and a wood stove look like a truck – I start trying to untangle hair. They only six and eight and they cry. They scream. They cuse me of murder. By ten o'clock I'm done. They cry theirselves to sleep. But I don't cry. I lay there thinking bout Nettie while he on top of me, wonder if she safe. And then I think bout Shug Avery. I know what he doing to me he done to Shug Avery and maybe she like it. I put my arm around him.

Dear God,

I was in town sitting on the wagon while Mr —— was in the dry good store. I seen my baby girl. I knowed it was her. She look just like me and my daddy. Like more us then us is ourself. She be tagging long hind a lady and they be dress just alike. They pass the wagon and I speak. The lady speak pleasant. My little girl she look up and sort of frown. She fretting over something. She got my eyes just like they is today. Like everything I seen, she seen, and she pondering it.

I think she mine. My heart say she mine. But I don't know she mine. If she mine, her name Olivia. I embroder Olivia in the seat of all her daidies. I embroder lot of little stars and flowers too. He took the daidies when he took her. She was bout two month old. Now she bout six.

I clam down from the wagon and I follow Olivia and her new mammy into a store. I watch her run her hand long side the counter, like she ain't interested in nothing. Her ma is buying cloth. She say Don't touch nothing. Olivia yawn.

That real pretty, I say, and help her mama drape a piece of cloth close to her face.

She smile. Gonna make me an my girl some new dresses, she say. Her daddy be so proud.

Who her daddy, I blurt out. It like *at last* somebody know.

She say Mr ——. But that ain't my daddy name.

Mr ——? I say. Who he?

She look like I ast something none of my bidniss.

The *Reverend* Mr ——, she say, then turn her face to the

clerk. He say, Girl you want that cloth or not? We got other customers sides you.

She say, Yes sir. I want five yards, please sir.

He snatch the cloth and thump down the bolt. He don't measure. When he think he got five yard he tare it off. That be a dollar and thirty cent, he say. You need thread?

She say, Naw suh.

He say, You can't sew thout thread. He pick up a spool and hold it gainst the cloth. That look like it bout the right color. Don't you think.

She say, Yessuh.

He start to whistle. Take two dollars. Give her a quarter back. He look at me. You want something gal? I say, Naw Suh.

I trail long behind them on the street.

I don't have nothing to offer and I feels poor.

She look up and down the street. He ain't here. He ain't here. She say like she gon cry.

Who ain't? I ast.

The Reverend Mr ——, she say. He took the wagon.

My husband wagon right here, I say.

She clam up. I thank you kindly, she say. Us sit looking at all the folks that's come to town. I never seen so many even at church. Some be dress too. Some don't hit on much. Dust git all up the ladies dress.

She ast me Who is my husband, now I know all bout hers. She laugh a little. I say Mr ——. She say, Sure nuff? Like she know all about him. Just didn't know he was married. He a fine looking man, she say. Not a finer looking one in the county. White or black, she say.

He do look all right, I say. But I don't think about it while I say it. Most times mens look pretty much alike to me.

How long you had your little girl? I ast.

Oh, she be seven her next birthday.

When that? I ast.

She think back. Then she say, December.

I think, November.

I say, real easy, What you call her?

She say, oh, we calls her Pauline.

My heart knock.

Then she frown. But *I* calls her Olivia.

Why you call her Olivia if it ain't her name? I ast.

Well, just look at her, she say sort of impish, turning to look at the child, don't she look like a Olivia to you? Look at her eyes, for god's sake. Somebody ole would have eyes like that. So I call her *ole* Livia. She chuckle. Naw. Olivia, she say, patting the child hair. Well, here come the Reverend Mr ———, she say. I see a wagon and a great big man in black holding a whip. We sure do thank you for your hospitality. She laugh again, look at the horses flicking flies off they rump. *Horse*pitality, she say. And I git it and laugh. It feel like to split my face.

Mr ———, come out the store. Clam up in the wagon. Set down. Say real slow. What you setting here laughing like a fool fer?

Dear God,

Nettie here with us. She run way from home. She say she hate to leave our stepma, but she had to git out, maybe fine help for the other little ones. The boys be alright, she say. They can stay out his way. When they git big they gon fight him.

Maybe kill, I say.

How is it with you and Mr ——? she ast. But she got eyes. He still like her. In the evening he come out on the porch in his Sunday best. She be sitting there with me shelling peas or helping the children with they spelling. Helping me with spelling and everything else she think I need to know. No matter what happen, Nettie steady try to teach me what go on in the world. And she a good teacher too. It nearly kill me to think she might marry somebody like Mr —— or wind up in some white lady kitchen. All day she read, she study, she practice her handwriting, and try to git us to think. Most days I feel too tired to think. But Patient her middle name.

Mr —— children all bright but they mean. They say Celie, I want dis. Celie, I want dat. Our Mama let us have it. He don't say nothing. They try to get his tension, he hide hind a puff of smoke.

Don't let them run over you, Nettie say. You got to let them know who got the upper hand.

They got it, I say.

But she keep on. You got to fight. You got to fight.

But I don't know how to fight. All I know how to do is stay alive.

*

That's a real pretty dress you got on, he say to Nettie.

She say, Thank you.

Them shoes look just right.

She say, Thank you.

Your skin. Your hair. Your teefs. Everyday it something else to make miration over.

First she smile a little. Then she frown. Then she don't look no special way at all. She just stick close to me. She tell me, Your skin. Your hair. Your teefs. He try to give her a compliment, she pass it on to me. After while I git to feeling pretty cute.

Soon he stop. He say one night in bed, Well, us done help Nettie all we can. Now she got to go.

Where she gon go? I ast.

I don't care, he say.

I tell Nettie the next morning. Stead of being mad, she glad to go. Say she hate to leave me is all. Us fall on each other neck when she say that.

I sure hate to leave you here with these rotten children, she say. Not to mention with Mr ———. It's like seeing you buried, she say.

It's worse than that, I think. If I was buried, I wouldn't have to work. But I just say, Never mine, never mine, long as I can spell G-o-d I got somebody along.

But I only got one thing to give her, the name of Reverend Mr ———. I tell her to ast for his wife. That maybe she would help. She the only woman I ever seen with money.

I say, Write.

She say, What?

I say, Write.

She say, Nothing but death can keep me from it.

She never write.

G-o-d,

Two of his sister come to visit. They dress all up. Celie, they say. One thing is for sure. You keep a clean house. It not nice to speak ill of the dead, one say, but the truth never can *be* ill. Annie Julia was a nasty 'oman bout the house.

She never want to be here in the first place, say the other.

Where she want to be? I ast.

At home. She say.

Well that's no excuse, say the first one, Her name Carrie, other one name Kate. When a woman marry she spose to keep a decent house and a clean family. Why, wasn't nothing to come here in the winter time and all these children have colds, they have flue, they have direar, they have newmonya, they have worms, they have the chill and fever. They hungry. They hair ain't comb. They too nasty to touch.

I touch 'em. Say Kate.

And cook. She wouldn't cook. She act like she never seen a kitchen.

She hadn't never seen his.

Was a scandal, say Carrie.

He sure was, say Kate.

What you mean? say Carrie.

I mean he just brought her here, dropped her, and kept right on running after Shug Avery. That what I mean. Nobody to talk to, nobody to visit. He be gone for days. Then she start having babies. And she young and pretty.

Not so pretty, say Carrie, looking in the looking glass. Just that head of hair. She too black.

Well, brother must like black. Shug Avery black as my shoe.

Shug Avery, Shug Avery, Carrie say. I'm sick of her. Somebody say she going round trying to sing. Umph, what she got to sing about. Say she wearing dresses all up her leg and headpieces with little balls and tassles hanging down, look like window dressing.

My ears perk up when they mention Shug Avery. I feel like I want to talk about her my own self. They hush.

I'm sick of her too, say Kate, letting out her breath. And you right about Celie, here. Good housekeeper, good with children, good cook. Brother couldn't have done better if he tried.

I think about how he tried.

This time Kate come by herself. She maybe twenty-five. Old maid. She look younger than me. Healthy. Eyes bright. Tongue sharp.

Buy Celie some clothes. She say to Mr ———.

She need clothes? he ast.

Well look at her.

He look at me. It like he looking at the earth. It need somethin? his eyes say.

She go with me in the store. I think what color Shug Avery would wear. She like a queen to me so I say to Kate, Somethin purple, maybe little red in it too. But us look an look and no purple. Plenty red but she say, Naw, he won't want to pay for red. Too happy lookin. We got choice of brown, maroon or navy blue. I say blue.

I can't remember being the first one in my own dress. Now to have one made just for me. I try to tell Kate what it mean. I git hot in the face and stutter.

She say. It's all right, Celie. You deserve more than this. Maybe so. I think.

Harpo, she say. Harpo the oldest boy. Harpo, don't let Celie be the one bring in all the water. You a big boy now. Time for you to help out some.

Women work, he say.

What? she say.

Women work. I'm a man.

You're a trifling nigger, she say. You git that bucket and bring it back full.

He cut his eye at me. Stumble out. I hear him mutter somethin to Mr —— sitting on the porch. Mr —— call his sister. She stay out on the porch talking a little while, then she come back in, shaking.

Got to go, Celie, she say.

She so mad tears be flying every which way while she pack.

You got to fight them, Celie, she say. I can't do it for you. You got to fight them for yourself.

I don't say nothing. I think bout Nettie, dead. She fight, she run away. What good it do? I don't fight, I stay where I'm told. But I'm alive.

Dear God,

Harpo ast his daddy why he beat me. Mr —— say, Cause she my wife. Plus, she stubborn. All women good for – he don't finish. He just tuck his chin over the paper like he do. Remind me of Pa.

Harpo ast me, How come you stubborn? He don't ast How come you his wife? Nobody ast that.

I say, Just born that way, I reckon.

He beat me like he beat the children. Cept he don't never hardly beat them. He say, Celie, git the belt. The children be outside the room peeking through the cracks. It all I can do not to cry. I make myself wood. I say to myself, Celie, you a tree. That's how come I know trees fear man.

Harpo say, I love Somebody.

I say, Huh?

He say, A Girl.

I say, You do?

He say, Yeah. Us plan to marry.

Marry, I say. You not old enough to marry.

I is, he say. I'm seventeen. She fifteen. Old enough.

What her mama say, I ast.

Ain't talk to her mama.

What her daddy say?

Ain't talk to him neither.

Well, what *she* say?

Us ain't never spoke. He duck his head. He ain't so bad looking. Tall and skinny, black like his mama, with great big bug eyes.

Where yall see each other? I ast. I see her in church, he say. She see me outdoors.

She like you?

I don't know. I wink at her. She act like she scared to look.

Where her daddy at while all this going on?

Amen corner, he say.

Dear God,

Shug Avery is coming to town! She coming with her orkestra. She going to sing in the Lucky Star out on Coalman road. Mr —— going to hear her. He dress all up in front the glass, look at himself, then undress and dress all over again. He slick back his hair with pomade, then wash it out again. He been spitting on his shoes and hitting it with a quick rag.

He tell me, Wash this. Iron that. Look for this. Look for that. Find this. Find that. He groan over holes in his sock.

I move round darning and ironing, finding hanskers. Anything happening? I ast.

What you mean? he say, like he mad. Just trying to git some of the hick farmer off myself. Any other woman be glad.

I is glad, I say.

What you mean? he ast.

You looks nice, I say. Any woman be proud.

You think so? he say.

First time he ast me. I'm so surprise, by time I say Yeah, he out on the porch, trying to shave where the light better.

I walk round all day with the announcement burning a hole in my pocket. It pink. The trees tween the turn off to our road and the store is lit up with them. He got bout five dozen in his trunk.

Shug Avery standing upside a piano, elbow crook, hand on her hip. She wearing a hat like Indian Chiefs. Her mouth open showing all her teef and don't nothing seem to be troubling her mind. Come one, come all, it say. The Queen Honeybee is back in town.

Lord, I wants to go so bad. Not to dance. Not to drink. Not to play card. Not even to hear Shug Avery sing. I just be thankful to lay eyes on her.

Dear God,

Mr —— be gone all night Saturday, all night Sunday and most all day Monday. Shug Avery in town for the weekend. He stagger in, throw himself on the bed. He tired. He sad. He weak. He cry. Then he sleep the rest of the day and all night.

He wake up while I'm in the field. I been chopping cotton three hours by time he come. Us don't say nothing to each other.

But I got a million question to ast. What she wear? Is she still the same old Shug, like in my picture? How her hair is? What kind lipstick? Wig? She stout? She skinny? She sound well? Tired? Sick? Where you all children at while she singing all over the place? Do she miss 'em? Questions be running back and forth through my mind. Feel like snakes. I pray for strength, bite the insides of my jaws.

Mr —— pick up a hoe and start to chop. He chop bout three chops then he don't chop again. He drop the hoe in the furrow, turn right back on his heel, walk back to the house, go git him a cool drink of water, git his pipe, sit on the porch and stare. I follow cause I think he sick. Then he say, You better git on back to the field. Don't wait for me.

Dear God,

Harpo no better at fighting his daddy back than me. Every day his daddy git up, sit on the porch, look out at nothing. Sometime look at the trees out front the house. Look at a butterfly if it light on the rail. Drink a little water in the day. A little wine in the evening. But mostly never move.

Harpo complain bout all the plowing he have to do.

His daddy say, You gonna do it.

Harpo nearly big as his daddy. He strong in body but weak in will. He scared.

Me and him out in the field all day. Us sweat, chopping and plowing. I'm roasted coffee bean color now. He black as the inside of a chimney. His eyes be sad and thoughtful. His face begin to look like a woman face.

Why you don't work no more? he ast his daddy.

No reason for me to. His daddy say. You here, ain't you? He say this nasty. Harpos feeling be hurt.

Plus, he still in love.

≈ 28 ≈

Dear God,

Harpo girl daddy say Harpo not good enough for her. Harpo been courting the girl a while. He say he sit in the parlor with her, the daddy sit right there in the corner till everybody feel terrible. Then he go sit on the porch in front the open door where he can hear everything. Nine o'clock come, he bring Harpo his hat.

Why I'm not good enough? Harpo ast Mr ———. Mr ——— say, Your mammy.

Harpo say, What wrong with my mammy?

Mr ——— say, Somebody kill her.

Harpo be trouble with nightmares. He see his mama running cross the pasture trying to git home. Mr ———, the man they say her boyfriend, catch up with her. She got Harpo by the hand. They both running and running. He grab hold of her shoulder, say, You can't quit me now. You mine. She say, No I ain't. My place is with my children. He say, Whore, you ain't got no place. He shoot her in the stomach. She fall down. The man run. Harpo grab her in his arms, put her head in his lap.

He start to call, Mama, Mama. It wake me up. The other children too. They cry like they mama just die. Harpo come to, shaking.

I light the lamp and stand over him, patting his back.

It not her fault somebody kill her, he say. It not! It not!

Naw, I say. It not.

*

Everybody say how good I is to Mr —— children. I be good to them. But I don't feel nothing for them. Patting Harpo back not even like patting a dog. It more like patting another piece of wood. Not a living tree, but a table, a chifferobe. Anyhow, they don't love me neither, no matter how good I is.

They don't mind. Cept for Harpo they won't work. The girls face always to the road. Bub be out all times of night drinking with boys twice his age. They daddy puff on his pipe.

Harpo tell me all his love business now. His mind on Sofia Butler day and night.

She pretty, he tell me. Bright.

Smart?

Naw. Bright *skin*. She smart too though, I think. Sometime us can git her away from her daddy.

I know right then the next thing I hear, she be big.

If she so smart how come she big? I ast.

Harpo shrug. She can't git out the house no other way, he say. Mr —— won't let us marry. Say I'm not good enough to come in his parlor. But if she big I got a right to be with her, good enough or no.

Where yall gon stay?

They got a big place, he say. When us marry I'll be just like one of the family.

Humph, I say. Mr —— didn't like you before she big, he ain't gonna like you *cause* she big.

Harpo look trouble.

Talk to Mr ——, I say. He your daddy. Maybe he got some good advice.

Maybe not. I think.

Harpo bring her over to meet his daddy. Mr —— say he want to have a look at her. I see 'em coming way off up the road. They be just marching, hand in hand, like going to war. She in front a little. They come up on the porch, I speak and move some chairs closer to the railing. She sit down and start to fan herself with a hansker. It sure is hot, she say. Mr ——— don't say nothing. He just look her up and down. She bout seven or eight months pregnant, bout to bust out her dress. Harpo so black he think she bright, but she ain't that bright. Clear medium brown skin, gleam on it like on good furniture. Hair notty but a lot of it, tied up on her head in a mass of plaits. She not quite as tall as Harpo but much bigger, and strong and ruddy looking, like her mama brought her up on pork.

She say, How you, Mr ———?

He don't answer the question. He say, Look like you done got yourself in trouble.

Naw suh, she say. I ain't in no trouble. Big, though.

She smooth the wrinkles over her stomach with the flats of her hands.

Who the father? he ast.

She look surprise. Harpo, she say.

How he know that?

He know. She say.

Young womens no good these days, he say. Got they legs open to every Tom, Dick and Harry.

Harpo look at his daddy like he never seen him before. But he don't say nothing.

Mr ——— say, No need to think I'm gon let my boy marry you just cause you in the family way. He young and limited. Pretty gal like you could put anything over on him.

Harpo still don't say nothing.

Sofia face git more ruddy. The skin move back on her forehead. Her ears raise.

But she laugh. She glance at Harpo sitting there with his head down and his hands tween his knees.

She say, What I need to marry Harpo for? He still living here with you. What food and clothes he git, you buy.

He say, Your daddy done throwed you out. Ready to live in the street I guess.

She say, Naw. I ain't living in the street. I'm living with my sister and her husband. They say I can live with them for the rest of my life. She stand up, big, strong, healthy girl, and she say, Well, nice visiting. I'm going home.

Harpo get up to come too. She say, Naw, Harpo, you stay here. When you free, me and the baby be waiting.

He sort of hang there between them a while, then he sit down again. I look at her face real quick then, and seem like a shadow go cross it. Then she say to me, Mrs ——, I'd thank you for a glass of water before I go, if you don't mind.

The bucket on the shelf right there on the porch. I git a clean glass out the safe and dip her up some water. She drink it down, almost in one swallow. Then she run her hands over her belly again and she take off. Look like the army change direction, and she heading off to catch up.

Harpo never git up from his chair. Him and his daddy sit there and sit there and sit there. They never talk. They never move. Finally I have supper and go to bed. I git up in the morning it feel like they still sitting there. But Harpo be in the outhouse, Mr —— be shaving.

Dear God,

Harpo went and brought Sofia and the baby home. They got married in Sofia sister house. Sister's husband stand up with Harpo. Other sister sneak way from home to stand up with Sofia. Another sister come to hold the baby. Say he cry right through the service, his mama stop everything to nurse him. Finish saying I do with a big ole nursing boy in her arms.

Harpo fix up the little creek house for him and his family. Mr —— daddy used it for a shed. But it sound. Got windows now, a porch, back door. Plus it cool and green down by the creek.

He ast me to make some curtains and I make some out of flower sack. It not big, but it homey. Got a bed, a dresser, a looking glass, and some chairs. Cookstove for cooking and heating, too. Harpo daddy give him wages for working now. He say Harpo wasn't working hard like he should. Maybe little money goose his interest.

Harpo told me, Miss Celie, I'm going on strike.

On what?

I ain't going to work.

And he don't. He come to the field, pull two ears of corn, let the birds and weevil eat two hundred. Us don't make nothing much this year.

But now Sofia coming, he always busy. He chop, he hammer, he plow. He sing and whistle.

Sofia look half her size. But she still a big strong girl. Arms got muscle. Legs, too. She swing that baby about like it nothing. She got a little pot on her now and give you the feeling she all there. Solid. Like if she sit down on something, it be mash.

She tell Harpo, Hold the baby, while she come back in the house with me to git some thread. She making some sheets. He take the baby, give it a kiss, chuck it under it chin. Grin, look up on the porch at his daddy.

Mr ——— blow smoke, look down at him, and say, Yeah, I see now she going to switch the traces on you.

Dear God,

Harpo want to know what to do to make Sofia mind. He sit out on the porch with Mr ———. He say, I tell her one thing, she do another. Never do what I say. Always backtalk.

To tell the truth, he sound a little proud of this to me.

Mr ——— don't say nothing. Blow smoke.

I tell her she can't be all the time going to visit her sister. Us married now, I tell her. Your place is here with the children. She say, I'll take the children with me. I say, Your place is with me. She say, You want to come? She keep primping in front the glass, getting the children ready at the same time.

You ever hit her? Mr ——— ast.

Harpo look down at his hands. Naw suh, he say low, embarrass.

Well how you specs to make her mind? Wives is like children. You have to let 'em know who got the upper hand. Nothing can do that better than a good sound beating.

He puff on his pipe.

Sofia think too much of herself anyway, he say. She need to be taken down a peg.

I like Sofia, but she don't act like me at all. If she talking when Harpo and Mr ——— come in the room, she keep right on. If they ast her where something at, she say she don't know. Keep talking.

I think bout this when Harpo ast me what he ought to do to her to make her mind. I don't mention how happy he is now. How three years pass and he still whistle and sing. I think bout how every time I jump when Mr —— call me, she look surprise. And like she pity me.

Beat her. I say.

Next time us see Harpo his face a mess of bruises. His lip cut. One of his eyes shut like a fist. He walk stiff and say his teef ache.

I say, What happen to you, Harpo?

He say, Oh, me and that mule. She fractious, you know. She went crazy in the field the other day. By time I got her to head for home I was all banged up. Then when I got home, I walked smack dab into the crib door. Hit my eye and scratch my chin. Then when that storm come up last night I shet the window down on my hand.

Well, I say, After all that, I don't specs you had a chance to see if you could make Sofia mind.

Nome, he say.

But he keep trying.

Dear God,

Just when I was bout to call out that I was coming in the yard, I hear something crash. It come from inside the house, so I run up on the porch. The two children be making mud pies on the edge of the creek, they don't even look up.

I open the door cautious, thinking bout robbers and murderers. Horsethieves and hants. But it Harpo and Sofia. They fighting like two mens. Every piece of furniture they got is turned over. Every plate look like it broke. The looking glass hang crooked, the curtains torn. The bed look like the stuffing pulled out. They don't notice. They fight. He try to slap her. What he do that for? She reach down and grab a piece of stove wood and whack him cross the eyes. He punch her in the stomach, she double over groaning but come up with both hands lock right under his privates. He roll on the floor. He grab her dress tail and pull. She stand there in her slip. She never blink a eye. He jump up to put a hammer lock under her chin, she throw him over her back. He fall *bam* up gainst the stove.

I don't know how long this been going on. I don't know when they specs to conclude. I ease on back out, wave to the children by the creek, walk back on up home.

Saturday morning early, us hear the wagon. Harpo, Sofia, the two babies be going off for the weekend, to visit Sofia sister.

Dear God,

For over a month I have trouble sleeping. I stay up late as I can before Mr —— start complaining bout the price of kerosene, then I soak myself in a warm bath with milk and epsom salts, then sprinkle little witch hazel on my pillow and curtain out all the moonlight. Sometimes I git a few hours sleep. Then just when it look like it ought to be gitting good, I wakes up.

At first I'd git up quick and drink some milk. Then I'd think bout counting fence post. Then I'd think bout reading the Bible.

What it is? I ast myself.

A little voice say, Something you done wrong. Somebody spirit you sin against. Maybe.

Way late one night it come to me. Sofia. I sin against Sofia spirit.

I pray she don't find out, but she do.

Harpo told.

The minute she hear it she come marching up the path, toting a sack. Little cut all blue and red under her eye.

She say, Just want you to know I looked to you for help.

Ain't I been helpful? I ast.

She open up her sack. Here your curtains, she say. Here your thread. Here a dollar for letting me use 'em.

They yourn, I say, trying to push them back. I'm glad to help out. Do what I can.

You told Harpo to beat me, she said.

No I didn't, I said.

Don't lie, she said.

I didn't mean it, I said.

Then what you say it for? she ast.

She standing there looking me straight in the eye. She look tired and her jaws full of air.

I say it cause I'm a fool, I say. I say it cause I'm jealous of you. I say it cause you do what I can't.

What that? she say.

Fight. I say.

She stand there a long time, like what I said took the wind out her jaws. She mad before, sad now.

She say, All my life I had to fight. I had to fight my daddy. I had to fight my brothers. I had to fight my cousins and my uncles. A girl child ain't safe in a family of men. But I never thought I'd have to fight in my own house. She let out her breath. I loves Harpo, she say. God knows I do. But I'll kill him dead before I let him beat me. Now if you want a dead son-in-law you just keep on advising him like you doing. She put her hand on her hip. I used to hunt game with a bow and arrow, she say.

I stop the little trembling that started when I saw her coming. I'm *so* shame of myself, I say. And the Lord he done whip me little bit too.

The Lord don't like ugly, she say.

And he ain't stuck on pretty.

This open the way for our talk to turn another way.

I say, You feels sorry for me, don't you?

She think a minute. Yes ma'am, she say slow, I do.

I think I know how come, but I ast her anyhow.

She say, To tell the truth, you remind me of my mama. She under my daddy thumb. Naw, she under my daddy foot. Anything he say, goes. She never say nothing back. She never stand up for herself. Try to make a little half stand sometime for the children but that always backfire. More she stand up for us, the harder time he give her. He hate children and he hate where they come from. Tho from all the children he got, you'd never know it.

I never know nothing bout her family. I thought, looking at her, nobody in her family could be scared.

How many he got? I ast.

Twelve. She say.

Whew, I say. My daddy got six by my mama before she die, I say. He got four more by the wife he got now. I don't mention the two he got by me.

How many girls? she ast.

Five, I say. How bout in your family?

Six boys, six girls. All the girls big and strong like me. Boys big and strong too, but all the girls stick together. Two brothers stick with us too, sometime. Us git in a fight, it's a sight to see.

I ain't never struck a living thing, I say. Oh, when I was at home I tap the little ones on the behind to make 'em behave, but not hard enough to hurt.

What you do when you git mad? she ast.

I think. I can't even remember the last time I felt mad, I say. I used to git mad at my mammy cause she put a lot of work on me. Then I see how sick she is. Couldn't stay mad at her. Couldn't be mad at my daddy cause he my daddy. Bible say, Honor father and mother no matter what. Then after while every time I got mad, or start to feel mad, I got sick. Felt like throwing up. Terrible feeling. Then I start to feel nothing at all.

Sofia frown. Nothing at all?

Well, sometime Mr —— git on me pretty hard. I have to talk to Old Maker. But he my husband. I shrug my shoulders. This life soon be over, I say. Heaven last all ways.

You ought to bash Mr —— head open, she say. Think bout heaven later.

Not much funny to me. That funny. I laugh. She laugh. Then us both laugh so hard us flop down on the step.

Let's make quilt pieces out of these messed up curtains, she say. And I run git my pattern book.

I sleeps like a baby now.

Dear God,

Shug Avery sick and nobody in this town want to take the Queen Honeybee in. Her mammy say She told her so. Her pappy say, Tramp. A woman at church say she dying – maybe two berkulosis or some kind of nasty woman disease. What? I want to ast, but don't. The women at church sometime nice to me. Sometime not. They look at me there struggling with Mr —— children. Trying to drag 'em to the church, trying to keep 'em quiet after us get there. They some of the same ones used to be here both times I was big. Sometimes they think I don't notice, they stare at me. Puzzle.

I keep my head up, best I can. I do a right smart for the preacher. Clean the floor and windows, make the wine, wash the altar linen. Make sure there's wood for the stove in wintertime. He call me Sister Celie. Sister Celie, he say, You faithful as the day is long. Then he talk to the other ladies and they mens. I scurry bout, doing this, doing that. Mr —— sit back by the door gazing here and there. The womens smile in his direction every chance they git. He never look at me or even notice.

Even the preacher got his mouth on Shug Avery, now she down. He take her condition for his text. He don't call no name, but he don't have to. Everybody know who he mean. He talk bout a strumpet in short skirts, smoking cigarettes, drinking gin. Singing for money and taking other women mens. Talk bout slut, hussy, heifer and streetcleaner.

I cut my eyes back at Mr —— when he say that. Streetcleaner. Somebody got to stand up for Shug, I think. But he don't say nothing. He cross his legs first to one side, then to the other. He gaze out the window. The same women smile at him, say amen gainst Shug.

But once us home he never stop to take off his clothes. He call down to Harpo and Sofia house. Harpo come running.

Hitch up the wagon, he say.

Where us going? say Harpo.

Hitch up the wagon, he say again.

Harpo hitch up the wagon. They stand there and talk a few minutes out by the barn. Then Mr —— drive off.

One good thing bout the way he never do any work round the place, us never miss him when he gone.

Five days later I look way off up the road and see the wagon coming back. It got sort of a canopy over it now, made out of old blankets or something. My heart begin to beat like furry, and the first thing I try to do is change my dress.

But too late for that. By time I git my head and arm out the old dress, I see the wagon pull up in the yard. Plus a new dress won't help none with my notty head and dusty headrag, my old everyday shoes and the way I smell.

I don't know what to do, I'm so beside myself. I stand there in the middle of the kitchen. Mind whirling. I feels like Who Would Have Thought.

Celie, I hear Mr —— call. *Harpo*.

I stick my head and my arm back in my old dress and wipe the sweat and dirt off my face as best I can. I come to the door. Yessir? I ast, and trip over the broom I was sweeping with when I first notice the wagon.

Harpo and Sofia in the yard now, looking inside the wagon. They faces grim.

Who this? Harpo ast.

The woman should have been your mammy, he say.

Shug Avery? Harpo ast. He look up at me.

Help me git her in the house, Mr —— say.

I think my heart gon fly out my mouth when I see one of her foots come poking out.

She not lying down. She climbing down tween Harpo and Mr ——. And she dress to kill. She got on a red wool dress and chestful of black beads. A shiny black hat with what look like chickinhawk feathers curve down side one cheek, and she carrying a little snakeskin bag, match her shoes.

She look so stylish it like the trees all round the house draw themself up tall for a better look. Now I see she stumble, tween the two men. She don't seem that well acquainted with her feets.

Close up I see all this yellow powder caked up on her face. Red rouge. She look like she ain't long for this world but dressed well for the next. But I know better.

Come on in, I want to cry. To shout. Come on in. With God help, Celie going to make you well. But I don't say nothing. It not my house. Also I ain't been told nothing.

They git halfway up the step, Mr —— look up at me. Celie, he say. This here Shug Avery. Old friend of the family. Fix up the spare room. Then he look down at her, hold her in one arm, hold on to the rail with the other. Harpo on the other side, looking sad. Sofia and the children in the yard, watching.

I don't move at once, cause I can't. I need to see her eyes. I feel like once I see her eyes my feets can let go the spot where they stuck.

Git moving, he say, sharp.

And then she look up.

Under all that powder her face black as Harpo. She got a long pointed nose and big fleshy mouth. Lips look like black plum. Eyes big, glossy. Feverish. And mean. Like, sick as she is, if a snake cross her path, she kill it.

She look me over from head to foot. Then she cackle. Sound like a death rattle. You sure *is* ugly, she say, like she ain't believed it.

Dear God,

Ain't nothing wrong with Shug Avery. She just sick. Sicker than anybody I ever seen. She sicker than my mama was when she die. But she more evil than my mama and that keep her alive.

Mr —— be in the room with her all time of the night or day. He don't hold her hand though. She too evil for that. Turn loose my goddam hand, she say to Mr ——. What the matter with you, you crazy? I don't need no weak little boy can't say no to his daddy hanging on me. I need me a man, she say. A man. She look at him and roll her eyes and laugh. It not much of a laugh but it keep him away from the bed. He sit over in the corner away from the lamp. Sometime she wake up in the night and don't even see. But he there. Sitting in the shadows chewing on his pipe. No tobacco in it. First thing she said, I don't want to smell no stinking blankety-blank pipe, you hear me, Albert?

Who Albert, I wonder. Then I remember Albert Mr —— first name.

Mr —— don't smoke. Don't drink. Don't even hardly eat. He just got her in that little room, watching every breath.

What happen to her I ast?

You don't want her here, just say so, he say. Won't do no good. But if that the way you feel . . . He don't finish.

I want her here, I say, too quick. He look at me like maybe I'm planning something bad.

I just want to know what happen, I say.

—≈ 45 ≈—

I look at his face. It tired and sad and I notice his chin weak. Not much chin there at all. I have more chin, I think. And his clothes dirty, dirty. When he pull them off, dust rise.

Nobody fight for Shug, he say. And a little water come to his eyes.

Dear God,

They have made three babies together but he squeamish bout giving her a bath. Maybe he figure he start thinking bout things he shouldn't. But what bout me? First time I got the full sight of Shug Avery long black body with it black plum nipples, look like her mouth, I thought I had turned into a man.

What you staring at? she ast. Hateful. She weak as a kitten. But her mouth just pack with claws. You never seen a naked woman before?

No ma'am, I said. I never did. Cept for Sofia, and she so plump and ruddy and crazy she feel like my sister.

She say, Well take a good look. Even if I is just a bag of bones now. She have the nerve to put one hand on her naked hip and bat her eyes at me. Then she suck her teef and roll her eyes at the ceiling while I wash her.

I wash her body, it feel like I'm praying. My hands tremble and my breath short.

She say, You ever have any kids?

I say, Yes ma'am.

She say, How many and don't you yes ma'am me, I ain't that old.

I say, two.

She ast me Where they is?

I say, I don't know.

She look at me funny.

My kids with they grandma, she say. She could stand the kids, I had to go.

You miss 'em? I ast.

Naw, she say. I don't miss nothing.

Dear God,

I ast Shug Avery what she want for breakfast. She say, What yall got? I say ham, grits, eggs, biscuits, coffee, sweet milk or butter milk, flapjacks. Jelly and jam.

She say, Is that all? What about orange juice, grapefruit, strawberries and cream. Tea. Then she laugh.

I don't want none of your damn food, she say. Just gimme a cup of coffee and hand me my cigarettes.

I don't argue. I git the coffee and light her cigarette. She wearing a long white gown and her thin black hand stretching out of it to hold the white cigarette looks just right. Something bout it, maybe the little tender veins I see and the big ones I try not to, make me scared. I feel like something pushing me forward. If I don't watch out I'll have hold of her hand, tasting her fingers in my mouth.

Can I sit in here and eat with you? I ast.

She shrug. She busy looking at a magazine. White women in it laughing, holding they beads out on one finger, dancing on top of motocars. Jumping into fountains. She flip the pages. Look dissatisfied. Remind me of a child trying to git something out a toy it can't work yet.

She drink her coffee, puff on her cigarette. I bite into a big juicy piece of home cured ham. You can smell this ham for a mile when you cooking it, it perfume up her little room with no trouble at all.

I lavish butter on a hot biscuit, sort of wave it about. I sop up ham gravey and splosh my eggs in with my grits.

She blow more and more smoke. Look down in her coffee like maybe its something solid at the bottom.

Finally she say, Celie, I believe I could drink a glass of water. And this here by the bed ain't fresh.

She hold out her glass.

I put my plate down on the card table by the bed. I go dip her up some water. I come back, pick up my plate. Look like a little mouse been nibbling the biscuit, a rat run off with the ham.

She act like nothing happen. Begin to complain bout being tired. Doze on off to sleep.

Mr —— ast me how I git her to eat.

I say, Nobody living can stand to smell home cured ham without tasting it. If they dead they got a chance. Maybe.

Mr —— laugh.

I notice something crazy in his eyes.

I been scared, he say. Scared. And he cover up his eyes with his hands.

Dear God,

Shug Avery sit up in bed a little today. I wash and comb out her hair. She got the nottiest, shortest, kinkiest hair I ever saw, and I loves every strand of it. The hair that come out in my comb I kept. Maybe one day I'll get a net, make me a rat to pomp up my own hair.

I work on her like she a doll or like she Olivia – or like she mama. I comb and pat, comb and pat. First she say, hurry up and git finish. Then she melt down a little and lean back gainst my knees. That feel just right, she say. That feel like mama used to do. Or maybe not mama. Maybe grandma. She reach for another cigarette. Start hum a little tune.

What that song? I ast. Sound low down dirty to me. Like what the preacher tell you its sin to hear. Not to mention sing.

She hum a little more. Something come to me, she say. Something I made up. Something you help scratch out my head.

Dear God,

Mr —— daddy show up this evening. He a little short shrunk up man with a bald head and gold spectacles. He clear his throat a lot, like everything he say need announcement. Talk with his head leant to the side.

He come right to the point.

Just couldn't rest till you got her in your house, could you? he say, coming up the step.

Mr —— don't say nothing. Look out cross the railing at the trees, over the top of the well. Eyes rest on the top of Harpo and Sofia house.

Won't you have a seat? I ast, pushing him up a chair. How bout a cool drink of water?

Through the window I hear Shug humming and humming, practicing her little song. I sneak back to her room and shet the window.

Old Mr —— say to Mr ——, Just what is it bout this Shug Avery anyway, he say. She black as tar, she nappy headed. She got legs like baseball bats.

Mr —— don't say nothing. I drop little spit in Old Mr —— water.

Why, say Old Mr ——, she ain't even clean. I hear she got the nasty woman disease.

I twirl the spit round with my finger. I think bout ground glass, wonder how you grind it. But I don't feel mad at all. Just interest.

Mr —— turn his head slow, watch his daddy drink. Then

say, real sad, You ain't got it in you to understand, he say. I love Shug Avery. Always have, always will. I should have married her when I had the chance.

Yeah, say Old Mr ——. And throwed your life away. (Mr —— grunt right there.) And a right smart of my money with it. Old Mr —— clear his throat. Nobody even sure exactly who her daddy is.

I never care who her daddy is, say Mr ——.

And her mammy take in white people dirty clothes to this day. Plus all her children got different daddys. It all just too trifling and confuse.

Well, say Mr —— and turn full face on his daddy, All Shug Avery children got the same daddy. I vouch for that.

Old Mr —— clear his throat. Well, this my house. This my land. Your boy Harpo in one of my houses, on my land. Weeds come up on my land, I chop 'em up. Trash blow over it I burn it. He rise to go. Hand me his glass. Next time he come I put a little Shug Avery pee in his glass. See how he like that.

Celie, he say, you have my sympathy. Not many women let they husband whore lay up in they house.

But he not saying this to me, he saying it to Mr ——.

Mr —— look up at me, our eyes meet. This the closest us ever felt.

He say, Hand Pa his hat, Celie.

And I do. Mr —— don't move from his chair by the railing. I stand in the door. Us watch Old Mr —— begin harrumping and harrumping down the road home.

Next one come visit, his brother Tobias. He real fat and tall, look like a big yellow bear. Mr —— small like his daddy, his brother stand way taller.

Where she at? he ast, grinning. Where the Queen Honey-bee? Got something for her, he say. He put little box of chocolate on the railing.

She sleeping, I say. Didn't sleep much last night.

How you doing there, Albert, he say, dragging up a chair. He run his hand over his slicked back hair and try to feel if there's a bugga in his nose. Wipe his hand on his pants. Shake out the crease.

I just heard Shug Avery was here, he say. How long you had her?

Oh, say Mr ——, couple of months.

Hell, say Tobias, I heard she was dying. That goes to show, don't it, that you can't believe everything you hear. He smooth down his mustache, run his tongue out the corners of his lips.

What you know good, Miss Celie? he say.

Not much, I say.

Me and Sofia piecing another quilt together. I got bout five squares pieced, spread out on the table by my knee. My basket full of scraps on the floor.

Always busy, always busy, he say. I wish Margaret was more like you. Save me a bundle of money.

Tobias and his daddy always talk bout money like they still got a lot. Old Mr —— been selling off the place so that nothing much left but the houses and the fields. My and Harpo fields bring in more than anybody.

I piece on my square. Look at the colors of the cloth.

Then I hear Tobias chair fall back and he say, *Shug*.

Shug halfway tween sick and well. Halfway tween good and evil, too. Most days now she show me and Mr —— her good side. But evil all over her today. She smile, like a razor opening. Say, Well, well, look who's here *today*.

She wearing a little flowery shift I made for her and nothing else. She look bout ten with her hair all cornrowed. She skinny as a bean, and her face full of eyes.

Me and Mr —— both look up at her. Both move to help her sit down. She don't look at him. She pull up a chair next to me.

She pick up a random piece of cloth out the basket. Hold it up to the light. Frown. How you sew this damn thing? she say.

I hand her the square I'm working on, start another one. She sew long crooked stiches, remind me of that little crooked tune she sing.

That real good, for first try, I say. That just fine and dandy. She look at me and snort. Everything I do is fine and dandy to you, Miss Celie, she say. But that's cause you ain't got good sense. She laugh. I duck my head.

She got a heap more than Margaret, say Tobias. Margaret take that needle and sew your nostrils together.

All womens not alike, Tobias, she say. Believe it or not.

Oh, I believe it, he say. Just can't prove it to the world.

First time I think about the world.

What the world got to do with anything, I think. Then I see myself sitting there quilting tween Shug Avery and Mr ———. Us three set together gainst Tobias and his fly speck box of chocolate. For the first time in my life, I feel just right.

Dear God,

Me and Sofia work on the quilt. Got it frame up on the porch. Shug Avery donate her old yellow dress for scrap, and I work in a piece every chance I get. It a nice pattern call Sister's Choice. If the quilt turn out perfect, maybe I give it to her, if it not perfect, maybe I keep. I want it for myself, just for the little yellow pieces, look like stars, but not. Mr ——— and Shug walk up the road to the mailbox. The house quiet, cept for the flies. They swing through every now and then, drunk from eating and enjoying the heat, buzz enough to make me drowsy.

Sofia look like something on her mind, she just not sure what. She bend over the frame, sew a little while, then rear back in her chair and look out cross the yard. Finally she rest her needle, say, Why do people eat, Miss Celie, tell me that.

To stay alive, I say. What else? Course some folks eat cause food taste good to 'em. Then some is gluttons. They love to feel they mouth work.

Them the only reasons you can think of? she ast.

Well, sometime it might be a case of being undernourish, I say.

She muse. He not undernourish, she say.

Who ain't? I ast.

Harpo. She say.

Harpo?

He eating more and more every day.

Maybe he got a tape worm?

She frown. Naw, she say. I don't think it a tape worm. Tape worm make you hungry. Harpo eat when he ain't even hungry.

What, force it down? This hard to believe, but sometime you hear new things everyday. Not me, you understand, but some folk do say that.

Last night for supper he ate a whole pan of biscuits by himself.

Naw. I say.

He sure did. And had two big glasses of butter milk along with it. This was after supper was over, too. I was giving the children they baths, getting 'em ready for bed. He sposed to be washing the dishes. Stead of washing plates, he cleaning 'em with his mouth.

Well maybe he was extra hungry. Yall is been working hard.

Not that hard, she say. And this morning, for breakfast, darn if he didn't have six eggs. After all that food he look too sick to walk. When us got to the field I thought he was going to faint.

If Sofia say DARN something wrong. Maybe he don't want to wash dishes, I say. His daddy never wash a dish in his life.

You reckon? she say. He seem so much to love it. To tell the truth, he love that part of housekeeping a heap more 'en me. I rather be out in the fields or fooling with the animals. Even chopping wood. But he love cooking and cleaning and doing little things round the house.

He sure is a good cook, I say. Big surprise to me that he knew anything about it. He never cooked so much as a egg when he lived at home.

I bet he wanted to, she said. It seem so natural to him. But Mr ———. You know how he is.

Oh, he all right, I say.

You feeling yourself, Miss Celie? Sofia ast.

I mean, he all right in some things, not in others.

Oh, she say. Anyway, next time he come here, notice if he eat anything.

I notice what he eat all right. First thing, coming up the steps, I give him a close look. He still skinny, bout half Sofia size, but I see a little pot beginning under his overalls.

What you got to eat, Miss Celie? he say, going straight to the warmer and a piece of fried chicken, then on to the safe for a slice of blackberry pie. He stand by the table and munch, munch. You got any sweet milk? he ast.

Got clabber, I say.

He say, Well, I love clabber. And dip him out some.

Sofia must not be feeding you, I say.

Why you say that? he ast with his mouth full.

Well, it not that long after dinner and here you is hungry again.

He don't say nothing. Eat.

Course, I say, suppertime not too far off either. Bout three four hours.

He rummage through the drawer for a spoon to eat the clabber with. He see a slice of cornbread on the shelf back of the stove, he grab it and crumble it into the glass.

Us go back out on the porch and he put his foots up on the railing. Eat his clabber and cornbread with the glass near bout to his nose. Remind me of a hog at the troth.

Food tasting like food to you these days huh, I say, listening to him chew.

He don't say nothing. Eat.

I look out cross the yard. I see Sofia dragging a ladder and then lean it up gainst the house. She wearing a old pair of Harpo pants. Got her head tied up in a headrag. She clam up the ladder to the roof, begin to hammer in nails. Sound echo cross the yard like shots.

Harpo eat, watch her.

Then he belch. Say, Scuse me, Miss Celie. Take the glass and spoon back in the kitchen. Come out and say Bye.

No matter what happening now. No matter who come. No matter what they say or do, Harpo eat through it. Food on his mind morning, noon and night. His belly grow and grow, but the rest of him don't. He begin to look like he big.

When it due? us ast.

Harpo don't say nothing. Reach for another piece of pie.

Dear God,

Harpo staying with us this weekend. Friday night after Mr —— and Shug and me done gone to bed, I heard this somebody crying. Harpo sitting out on the steps, crying like his heart gon break. Oh, boo-hoo, and boo-hoo. He got his head in his hands, tears and snot running down his chin. I give him a hansker. He blow his nose, look up at me out of two eyes close like fists.

What happen to your eyes? I ast.

He clam round in his mind for a story to tell, then fall back on the truth.

Sofia, he say.

You still bothering Sofia? I ast.

She my wife, he say.

That don't mean you got to keep on bothering her, I say. Sofia love you, she a good wife. Good to the children and good looking. Hardworking. Godfearing and *clean*. I don't know what more you want.

Harpo sniffle.

I want her to do what I say, like you do for Pa.

Oh, Lord, I say.

When Pa tell you to do something, you do it, he say. When he say not to, you don't. You don't do what he say, he beat you.

Sometime beat me anyhow, I say, whether I do what he say or not.

That's right, say Harpo. But not Sofia. She do what she

want, don't pay me no mind at all. I try to beat her, she black my eyes. Oh, boo-hoo, he cry. Boo-hoo-hoo.

I start to take back my hansker. Maybe push him and his black eyes off the step. I think bout Sofia. She tickle me. I used to hunt game with a bow and arrow, she say.

Some womens can't be beat, I say. Sofia one of them. Besides, Sofia love you. She probably be happy to do most of what you say if you ast her right. She not mean, she not spiteful. She don't hold a grudge.

He sit there hanging his head, looking retard.

Harpo, I say, giving him a shake, Sofia *love* you. You *love* Sofia.

He look up at me best he can out his fat little eyes. Yes ma'am? he say.

Mr —— marry me to take care of his children. I marry him cause my daddy made me. I don't love Mr —— and he don't love me.

But you his wife, he say, just like Sofia mine. The wife spose to mind.

Do Shug Avery mind Mr ——? I ast. She the woman he wanted to marry. She call him Albert, tell him his drawers stink in a minute. Little as he is, when she git her weight back she can sit on him if he try to bother her.

Why I mention weight. Harpo start to cry again. Then he start to be sick. He lean over the edge of the step and vomit and vomit. Look like every piece of pie for the last year come up. When he empty I put him in the bed next to Shug's little room. He fall right off to sleep.

Dear God,

I go visit Sofia, she still working on the roof.

The darn thing leak, she say.

She out to the woodpile making shingles. She put a big square piece of wood on the chopping block and chop, chop, she make big flat shingles. She put the ax down and ast me do I want some lemonade.

I look at her good. Except for a bruise on her wrist, she don't look like she got a scratch on her.

How it going with you and Harpo? I ast.

Well, she say, he stop eating so much. But maybe this just a spell.

He trying to git as big as you, I say.

She suck in her breath. I kinda thought so, she say, and let out her breath real slow.

All the children come running up, Mama, Mama, us want lemonade. She pour out five glasses for them, two for us. Us sit in a wooden swing she made last summer and hung on the shady end of the porch.

I'm gitting tired of Harpo, she say. All he think about since us married is how to make me mind. He don't want a wife, he want a dog.

He your husband, I say. Got to stay with thim. Else, what you gon do?

My sister husband caught in the draft, she say. They don't have no children, Odessa love children. He left her on a little farm. Maybe I go stay with them a while. Me and my children.

I think bout my sister Nettie. Thought so sharp it go through me like a pain. Somebody to run to. It seem too sweet to bear.

Sofia go on, frowning at her glass.

I don't like to go to bed with him no more, she say. Used to be when he touch me I'd go all out my head. Now when he touch me I just don't want to be bothered. Once he git on top of me I think bout how that's where he always want to be. She sip her lemonade. I use to love that part of it, she say. I use to chase him home from the field. Git all hot just watching him put the children to bed. But no more. Now I feels tired all the time. No interest.

Now, now, I say. Sleep on it some, maybe it come back. But I say this just to be saying something. I don't know nothing bout it. Mr —— clam on top of me, do his business, in ten minutes us both sleep. Only time I feel something stirring down there is when I think bout Shug. And that like running to the end of the road and it turn back on itself.

You know the worst part? she say. The worst part is I don't think he notice. He git up there and enjoy himself just the same. No matter what I'm thinking. No matter what I feel. It just him. Heartfeeling don't even seem to enter into it. She snort. The fact he can do it like that make me want to kill him.

Us look up the path to the house, see Shug and Mr —— sitting on the steps. He reach over and pick something out her hair.

I don't know, say Sofia. Maybe I won't go. Deep down I still love Harpo, but – he just makes me *real* tired. She yawn. Laugh. I need a vacation, she say. Then she go back to the woodpile, start making some more shingles for the roof.

Dear God,

Sofia right about her sisters. They all big strong healthy girls, look like amazons. They come early one morning in two wagons to pick Sofia up. She don't have much to take, her and the children clothes, a mattress she made last winter, a looking glass and a rocking chair. The children.

Harpo sit on the steps acting like he don't care. He making a net for seining fish. He look out toward the creek every once in a while and whistle a little tune. But it nothing compared to the way he usually whistle. His little whistle sound like it lost way down in a jar, and the jar in the bottom of the creek.

At the last minute I decide to give Sofia the quilt. I don't know what her sister place be like, but we been having right smart cold weather long in now. For all I know, she and the children have to sleep on the floor.

You gon let her go? I ast Harpo.

He look like only a fool could ast the question. He puff back, She made up her mind to go, he say. How I'm gon stop her? Let her go on, he say, cutting his eyes at her sister wagons.

Us sit on the steps together. All us hear from inside is the thump, thump, thump of plump and stout feet. All Sofia sisters moving round together at one time make the house shake.

Where us going? ast the oldest girl.

Going to visit Aunt Odessa, say Sofia.

Daddy coming? she ast.

Naw, say Sofia.

How come daddy ain't coming? another one ast.

Daddy need to stay here and take care of the house. Look after Dilsey, Coco and Boo.

The child come stand in front of his daddy and just look at him real good.

You not coming? he say.

Harpo say, Naw.

Child go whisper to the baby crawling round on the floor, Daddy not coming with us, what you think of that.

Baby sit real still, strain real hard, fart.

Us all laugh, but it sad too. Harpo pick it up, finger the daidie, and get her ready for a change.

I don't think she wet, say Sofia. Just gas.

But he change her anyway. Him and the baby over in a corner of the little porch out of the way of traffic. He use the old dry daidie to wipe his eyes.

At the last, he hand Sofia the baby and she sling it up side her hip, sling a sack of daidies and food over her shoulder, corral all the little ones together, tell 'em to Say Good-bye to Daddy. Then she hug me best she can what with the baby and all, and she clam up on the wagon. Every sister just about got a child tween her knees, cept the two driving the mules, and they all quiet as they leave Sofia and Harpo yard and drive on up past the house.

Dear God,

Sofia gone six months, Harpo act like a different man. Used to be a homebody, now all the time in the road.

I ast him what going on. He say, Miss Celie, I done learned a few things.

One thing he learned is that he cute. Another that he smart. Plus, he can make money. He don't say who the teacher is.

I hadn't heard so much hammering since before Sofia left, but every evening after he leave the field, he knocking down and nailing up. Sometime his friend Swain come by to help. The two of them work all into the night. Mr —— have to call down to tell them to shut up the racket.

What you building? I ast.

Jukejoint, he say.

Way back here?

No further back than any of the others.

I don't know nothing bout no others, only bout the Lucky Star.

Jukejoint sposed to be back in the woods, say Harpo. Nobody be bothered by the loud music. The dancing. The fights.

Swain say, the killings.

Harpo say, and the polices don't know where to look.

What Sofia gon say bout what you doing to her house? I ast. Spose she and the children come back. Where they gon sleep.

They ain't coming back, say Harpo, nailing together planks for a counter.

How you know? I ast.

He don't answer. He keep working, doing every thing with Swain.

Dear God,

The first week, nobody come. Second week, three or four. Third week, one. Harpo sit behind his little counter listening to Swain pick his box.

He got cold drinks, he got barbecue, he got chitlins, got store bought bread. He got a sign saying Harpo's tacked up on the side of the house and another one out on the road. But he ain't got no customers.

I go down the path to the yard, stand outside, look in. Harpo look out and wave.

Come on in, Miss Celie, he say.

I say, Naw thank you.

Mr —— sometime walk down, have a cold drink, listen to Swain. Miss Shug walk down too, every once in a while. She still wearing her little shifts, and I still cornrow her hair, but it getting long now and she say soon she want it press.

Harpo puzzle by Shug. One reason is she say whatever come to mind, forgit about polite. Sometime I see him staring at her real hard when he don't think I'm looking.

One day he say, Nobody coming way out here just to hear Swain. Wonder could I get the Queen Honeybee?

I don't know, I said. She a lot better now, always humming or singing something. She probably be glad to git back to work. Why don't you ask her?

Shug say his place not much compared to what she used to, but she think maybe she might grace it with a song.

Harpo and Swain got Mr ——— to give 'em some of Shug old announcements from out the trunk. Crossed out The Lucky Star of Coalman Road, put in Harpo's of ——— plantation. Stuck 'em on trees tween the turn off to our road and town. The first Saturday night so many folks come they couldn't git in.

Shug, Shug baby, us thought you was dead.

Five out of a dozen say hello to Shug like that.

And come to find out it was you, Shug say with a big grin.

At last I git to see Shug Avery work. I git to watch her. I git to hear her.

Mr ——— didn't want me to come. Wives don't go to places like that, he say.

Yeah, but Celie going, say Shug, while I press her hair. Spose I git sick while I'm singing, she say. Spose my dress come undone? She wearing a skintight red dress look like the straps made out of two pieces of thread.

Mr ——— mutter, putting on his clothes. My wife can't do this. My wife can't do that. No wife of mines . . . He go on and on.

Shug Avery finally say, Good thing I ain't your damn wife.

He hush then. All three of us go down to Harpo's. Mr ——— and me sit at the same table. Mr ——— drink whiskey. I have a cold drink.

First Shug sing a song by somebody name Bessie Smith. She say Bessie somebody she know. Old friend. It call A Good Man Is Hard to Find. She look over at Mr ——— a little when she sing that. I look over at him too. For such a little man, he all puff up. Look like all he can do to stay in his chair. I look at Shug and I feel my heart begin to cramp. It hurt me so, I cover it with my hand. I think I might as well be under the table, for all they care. I hate the way I look, I hate the way I'm dress. Nothing but churchgoing clothes in my chifferobe. And Mr ——— looking at Shug's bright black skin in her tight red dress, her feet in little sassy red shoes. Her hair shining in waves.

Before I know it, tears meet under my chin.

And I'm confuse.

He love looking at Shug. I love looking at Shug.

But Shug don't love looking at but one of us. Him.

But that the way it spose to be. I know that. But if that so, why my heart hurt me so?

My head droop so it near bout in my glass.

Then I hear my name.

Shug saying Celie. Miss Celie. And I look up where she at.

She say my name again. She say this song I'm bout to sing is call Miss Celie's song. Cause she scratched it out of my head when I was sick.

First she hum it a little, like she do at home. Then she sing the words.

It all about some no count man doing her wrong, again. But I don't listen to that part. I look at her and I hum along a little with the tune.

First time somebody made something and name it after me.

Dear God,

Pretty soon it be time for Shug to go. She sing every weekend now at Harpo's. He make right smart money off of her, and she make some too. Plus she gitting strong again and stout. First night or two her songs come out good but a little weak, now she belt them out. Folks out in the yard hear her with no trouble. She and Swain sound real good together. She sing, he pick his box. It nice at Harpo's. Little tables all round the room with candles on them that I made, lot of little tables outside too, by the creek. Sometime I look down the path from our house and it look like a swarm of lightening bugs all in and through Sofia house. In the evening Shug can't wait to go down there.

One day she say to me, Well, Miss Celie, I believe it time for me to go.

When? I ast.

Early next month, she say. June. June a good time to go off into the world.

I don't say nothing. Feel like I felt when Nettie left.

She come over and put her hand on my shoulder.

He beat me when you not here, I say.

Who do, she say, Albert?

Mr ——, I say.

I can't believe it, she say. She sit down on the bench next to me real hard, like she drop.

What he beat you for? she ast.

For being me and not you.

Oh, Miss Celie, she say, and put her arms around me.

Us sit like that for maybe half a hour. Then she kiss me on the fleshy part of my shoulder and stand up.

I won't leave, she say, until I know Albert won't even think about beating you.

Dear God,

Now we all know she going sometime soon, they sleep together at night. Not every night, but almost every night, from Friday to Monday.

He go down to Harpo's to watch her sing. And just to look at her. Then way late they come home. They giggle and they talk and they rassle until morning. Then they go to bed until it time for her to get ready to go back to work.

First time it happen, it was a accident. Feeling just carried them away. That what Shug say. He don't say nothing.

She ast me, Tell me the truth, she say, do you mind if Albert sleep with me?

I think, I don't care who Albert sleep with. But I don't say that.

I say, You might git big again.

She say, Naw, not with my sponge and all.

You still love him, I ast.

She say, I got what you call a passion for him. If I was ever going to have a husband he'd a been it. But he weak, she say. Can't make up his mind what he want. And from what you tell me he a bully. Some things I love about him though, she say. He smell right to me. He so little. He make me laugh.

You like to sleep with him? I ast.

Yeah, Celie, she say, I have to confess, I just *love* it. Don't you?

Naw, I say. Mr —— can tell you, I don't like it at all.

What is it to like? He git up on you, heist your nightgown round your waist, plunge in. Most times I pretend I ain't there. He never know the difference. Never ast me how I feel, nothing. Just do his business, get off, go to sleep.

She start to laugh. Do his business, she say. Do his business. Why, Miss Celie. You make it sound like he going to the toilet on you.

That what it feel like, I say.

She stop laughing.

You never enjoy it at all? she ast, puzzle. Not even with your children daddy?

Never, I say.

Why Miss Celie, she say, you still a virgin.

What? I ast.

Listen, she say, right down there in your pussy is a little button that gits real hot when you do you know what with somebody. It git hotter and hotter and then it melt. That the good part. But other parts good too, she say. Lot of sucking go on, here and there, she say. Lot of finger and tongue work.

Button? Finger and *tongue*? My face hot enough to melt itself.

She say, Here, take this mirror and go look at yourself down there, I bet you never seen it, have you?

Naw.

And I bet you never seen Albert down there either.

I felt him, I say.

I stand there with the mirror.

She say, What, too shame even to go off and look at yourself? And you look so cute too, she say, laughing. All dressed up for Harpo's, smelling good and everything, but scared to look at your own pussy.

You come with me while I look, I say.

And us run off to my room like two little prankish girls.

You guard the door, I say.

She giggle. Okay, she say. Nobody coming. Coast clear.

I lie back on the bed and haul up my dress. Yank down my bloomers. Stick the looking glass tween my legs. Ugh. All that hair. Then my pussy lips be black. Then inside look like a wet rose.

It a lot prettier than you thought, ain't it? she say from the door.

It mine, I say. Where the button?

Right up near the top, she say. The part that stick out a little.

I look at her and touch it with my finger. A little shiver go through me. Nothing much. But just enough to tell me this the right button to mash. Maybe.

She say, While you looking, look at your titties too. I haul up my dress and look at my titties. Think bout my babies sucking them. Remember the little shiver I felt then too. Sometimes a big shiver. Best part about having the babies was feeding 'em.

Albert and Harpo coming, she say. And I yank up my drawers and yank down my dress. I feel like us been doing something wrong.

I don't care if you sleep with him, I say.

And she take me at my word.

I take me at my word too.

But when I hear them together all I can do is pull the quilt over my head and finger my little button and titties and cry.

Dear God,

One night while Shug singing a hot one, who should come prancing through the door of Harpo's but Sofia.

She with a big tall hefty man look like a prize fighter.

She her usual stout and bouncy self.

Oh, Miss Celie, she cry. It so good to see you again. It even good to see Mr ———, she say. She take one of his hands. Even if his handshake is a little weak, she say.

He act real glad to see her.

Here, pull up a chair, he say. Have a cold drink.

Gimme a shot of white lightening, she say.

Prizefighter pull up a chair, straddle it backwards, hug on Sofia like they at home.

I see Harpo cross the room with his little yellowskin girlfriend. He look at Sofia like she a hant.

This Henry Broadnax, Sofia say. Everybody call him Buster. Good friend of the family.

How you all? he say. He smile pleasant and us keep listening to the music. Shug wearing a gold dress that show her titties near bout to the nipple. Everybody sorta hoping something break. But that dress strong.

Man oh man, say Buster. Fire department won't do. Somebody call the Law.

Mr ——— whisper to Sofia. Where your children at?

She whisper back, My children at home, where yours?

He don't say nothing.

Both the girls bigged and gone. Bub in and out of jail. If

his granddaddy wasn't the colored uncle of the sheriff who look just like Bub, Bub be lynch by now.

I can't git over how good Sofia look.

Most women with five children look a little peaked, I say to her cross the table when Shug finish her song. You look like you ready for five more.

Oh, she say, I got six children now, Miss Celie.

Six. I am shock.

She toss her head, look over at Harpo. Life don't stop just cause you leave home, Miss Celie. You know that.

My life stop when I left home, I think. But then I think again. It stop with Mr —— maybe, but start up again with Shug.

Shug come over and she and Sofia hug.

Shug say, Girl, you look like a good time, you do.

That when I notice how Shug talk and act sometimes like a man. Men say stuff like that to women, Girl, you look like a good time. Women always talk bout hair and health. How many babies living or dead, or got teef. Not bout how some woman they hugging on look like a good time.

All the men got they eyes glued to Shug's bosom. I got my eyes glued there too. I feel my nipples harden under my dress. My little button sort of perk up too. Shug, I say to her in my mind, Girl, you looks like a real good time, the Good Lord knows you do.

What you doing here? ast Harpo.

Sofia say, Come to hear Miss Shug. You got a nice place here Harpo. She look around. This and that her eyes admire.

Harpo say, It just a scandless, a woman with five children hanging out in a jukejoint at night.

Sofia eye go cool. She look him up and down.

Since he quit stuffing himself, he gained a bunch of weight, face, head and all, mostly from drinking home brew and eating left-over barbecue. By now he just about her size.

A woman need a little fun, once in a while, she say.

A woman need to be at home, he say.

She say, This is my home. Though I do think it go better as a jukejoint.

Harpo look at the prize fighter. Prizefighter push back his chair a little, pick up his drink.

I don't fight Sofia battle, he say. My job to love her and take her where she want to go.

Harpo breathe some relief.

Let's dance, he say.

Sofia laugh, git up. Put both arms round his neck. They slow drag out cross the floor.

Harpo little yellowskin girlfriend sulk, hanging over the bar. She a nice girl, friendly and everything, but she like me. She do anything Harpo say.

He give her a little nickname, too, call her Squeak.

Pretty soon Squeak git up her nerve to try to cut in.

Harpo try to turn Sofia so she can't see. But Squeak keep on tapping and tapping on his shoulder.

Finally he and Sofia stop dancing. They bout two feet from our table.

Shug say, uh-oh, and point with her chin, something bout to blow right there.

Who dis woman, say Squeak, in this little teenouncy voice.

You know who she is, say Harpo.

Squeak turn to Sofia. Say, You better leave him alone.

Sofia say, Fine with me. She turn round to leave.

Harpo grab her by the arm. Say, You don't have to go no where. Hell, this your house.

Squeak say, What you mean, Dis her house? She walk out on you. Walk away from the house. It over now, she say to Sofia.

Sofia say, Fine with me. Try to pull away from Harpo grip. He hold her tight.

Listen Squeak, say Harpo, Can't a man dance with his own wife?

Squeak say, Not if he my man he can't. You hear that, bitch, she say to Sofia.

Sofia gitting a little tired of Squeak, I can tell by her ears. They sort of push back. But she say again, sorta end of argument like, Hey, fine with me.

Squeak slap her up cross the head.

What she do that for. Sofia don't even deal in little ladyish things such as slaps. She ball up her fist, draw back, and knock two of Squeak's side teef out. Squeak hit the floor. One toof hanging on her lip, the other one upside my cold drink glass.

Then Squeak start banging on Harpo leg with her shoe.

You git that bitch out a here, she cry, blood and slobber running down her chin.

Harpo and Sofia stand side by side looking down at Squeak, but I don't think they hear her. Harpo still holding Sofia arm. Maybe half a minute go by. Finally he turn loose her arm, reach down and cradle poor little Squeak in his arms. He coo and coo at her like she a baby.

Sofia come over and git the prizefighter. They go out the door and don't look back. Then us hear a car motor start.

Dear God,

Harpo mope. Wipe the counter, light a cigarette, look
outdoors, walk up and down. Little Squeak run long all up
under him trying to git his tension. Baby this, she say, Baby
that. Harpo look through her head, blow smoke.

Squeak come over to the corner where me and Mr ——
at. She got two bright gold teef in the side of her mouth,
generally grin all the time. Now she cry. Miss Celie, she say,
What the matter with Harpo?

Sofia in jail, I say.

In jail? She look like I say Sofia on the moon.

What she in jail for? she ast.

Sassing the mayor's wife, I say.

Squeak pull up a chair. Look down my throat.

What your real name? I ast her. She say, Mary Agnes.

Make Harpo call you by your real name, I say. Then
maybe he see you even when he trouble.

She look at me puzzle. I let it go. I tell her what one of
Sofia sister tell me and Mr ——.

Sofia and the prizefighter and all the children got in the
prizefighter car and went to town. Clam out on the street
looking like somebody. Just then the mayor and his wife
come by.

All these children, say the mayor's wife, digging in her
pocketbook. Cute as little buttons though, she say. She stop,
put her hand on one of the children head. Say, and such
strong white teef.

Sofia and the prizefighter don't say nothing. Wait for her to pass. Mayor wait too, stand back and tap his foot, watch her with a little smile. Now Millie, he say. Always going on over colored. Miss Millie finger the children some more, finally look at Sofia and the prizefighter. She look at the prizefighter car. She eye Sofia wristwatch. She say to Sofia, All your children so clean, she say, would you like to work for me, be my maid?

Sofia say, Hell no.

She say, What you say?

Sofia say, Hell no.

Mayor look at Sofia, push his wife out the way. Stick out his chest. Girl, what you say to Miss Millie?

Sofia say, I say, Hell no.

He slap her.

I stop telling it right there.

Squeak on the edge of her seat. She wait. Look down my throat some more.

No need to say no more, Mr —— say. You know what happen if somebody slap Sofia.

Squeak go white as a sheet. *Naw*, she say.

Naw nothing, I say. Sofia knock the man down.

The polices come, start slinging the children off the mayor, bang they heads together. Sofia really start to fight. They drag her to the ground.

This far as I can go with it, look like. My eyes git full of water and my throat close.

Poor Squeak all scrunch down in her chair, trembling.

They beat Sofia, Mr —— say.

Squeak fly up like she sprung, run over hind the counter to Harpo, put her arms round him. They hang together a long time, cry.

What the prizefighter do in all this? I ast Sofia sister, Odessa.

He want to jump in, she say. Sofia say No, take the children home.

Polices have they guns on him anyway. One move, he dead. Six of them, you know.

Mr —— go plead with the sheriff to let us see Sofia. Bub be in so much trouble, look so much like the sheriff, he and Mr —— almost on family terms. Just long as Mr —— know he colored.

Sheriff say, She a crazy woman, your boy's wife. You know that?

Mr —— say, Yassur, us do know it. Been trying to tell Harpo she crazy for twelve years. Since way before they marry. Sofia come from crazy peoples, Mr —— say, it not all her fault. And then again, the sheriff know how womens is, anyhow.

Sheriff think bout the women he know, say, Yep, you right there.

Mr —— say, We gon tell her she crazy too, if us ever do git in to see her.

Sheriff say, Well make sure you do. And tell her she lucky she alive.

When I see Sofia I don't know why she still alive. They crack her skull, they crack her ribs. They tear her nose loose on one side. They blind her in one eye. She swole from head to foot. Her tongue the size of my arm, it stick out tween her teef like a piece of rubber. She can't talk. And she just about the color of a eggplant.

Scare me so bad I near bout drop my grip. But I don't. I put it on the floor of the cell, take out comb and brush, nightgown, witch hazel and alcohol and I start to work on her. The colored tendant bring me water to wash her with, and I start at her two little slits for eyes.

Dear God,

They put Sofia to work in the prison laundry. All day long from five to eight she washing clothes. Dirty convict uniforms, nasty sheets and blankets piled way over her head. Us see her twice a month for half a hour. Her face yellow and sickly, her fingers look like fatty sausage.

Everything nasty here, she say, even the air. Food bad enough to kill you with it. Roaches here, mice, flies, lice and even a snake or two. If you say anything they strip you, make you sleep on a cement floor without a light.

How you manage? us ast.

Every time they ast me to do something, Miss Celie, I act like I'm you. I jump right up and do just what they say.

She look wild when she say that, and her bad eye wander round the room.

Mr —— suck in his breath. Harpo groan. Miss Shug cuss. She come from Memphis special to see Sofia.

I can't fix my mouth to say how I feel.

I'm a good prisoner, she say. Best convict they ever see. They can't believe I'm the one sass the mayor's wife, knock the mayor down. She laugh. It sound like something from a song. The part where everybody done gone home but you.

Twelve years a long time to be good though, she say.

Maybe you git out on good behavior, say Harpo.

Good behavior ain't good enough for them, say Sofia. Nothing less than sliding on your belly with your tongue on they boots can even git they attention. I dream of murder, she say, I dream of murder sleep or wake.

Us don't say nothing.

How the children? she ast.

They all fine, say Harpo. Tween Odessa and Squeak, they git by.

Say thank you to Squeak, she say. Tell Odessa I think about her.

Dear God,

Us all sit round the table after supper. Me, Shug, Mr ———, Squeak, the prizefighter, Odessa and two more of Sofia sisters.

Sofia not gon last, say Mr ———.

Yeah, say Harpo, she look little crazy to me.

And what she had to say, say Shug. My God.

Us got to do something, say Mr ——— and be right quick about it.

What can us do? ast Squeak. She look a little haggard with all Sofia and Harpo children sprung on her at once, but she carry on. Hair a little stringy, slip show, but she carry on.

Bust her out, say Harpo. Git some dynamite off the gang that's building that big bridge down the road, blow the whole prison to kingdom come.

Shut up, Harpo, say Mr ———, us trying to think.

I got it, say the prizefighter, smuggle in a gun. Well, he rub his chin, maybe smuggle in a file.

Naw, say Odessa. They just come after her if she leave that way.

Me and Squeak don't say nothing. I don't know what she think, but I think bout angels, God coming down by chariot, swinging down real low and carrying ole Sofia home. I see 'em all as clear as day. Angels all in white, white hair and white eyes, look like albinos. God all white too, looking like some stout white man work at the bank. Angels strike they cymbals, one of them blow his horn, God blow out a big breath of fire and suddenly Sofia free.

Who the warden's black kinfolks? say Mr ———.

Nobody say nothing.

Finally the prizefighter speak. What his name? he ast.

Hodges, say Harpo. Bubber Hodges.

Old man Henry Hodges' boy, say Mr ———. Used to live out on the old Hodges' place.

Got a brother name Jimmy? ast Squeak.

Yeah, say Mr ———. Brother name Jimmy. Married to that Quitman girl. Daddy own the hardware. You know them?

Squeak duck her head. Mumble something.

Say what? ast Mr ———.

Squeak cheek turn red. She mumble again.

He your what? Mr ——— ast.

Cousin, she say.

Mr ——— look at her.

Daddy, she say. She cut her eye at Harpo. Look at the floor.

He know anything bout it? ast Mr ———.

Yeah, she say. He got three children by my mama. Two younger than me.

His brother know anything bout it? ast Mr ———.

One time he come by the house with Mr Jimmy, he give us all quarters, say we sure do look like Hodges.

Mr ——— rear back in his chair, give Squeak a good look from head to foot. Squeak push her greasy brown hair back from her face.

Yeah, say Mr ———. I see the resemblance. He bring his chair down on the floor.

Well, look like you the one to go.

Go where, ast Squeak.

Go see the warden. He your uncle.

Dear God,

Us dress Squeak like she a white woman, only her clothes patch. She got on a starch and iron dress, high heel shoes with scuffs, and a old hat somebody give Shug. Us give her a old pocketbook look like a quilt and a little black bible. Us wash her hair and git all the grease out, then I put it up in two plaits that cross over her head. Us bathe her so clean she smell like a good clean floor.

What I'm gon say? she ast.

Say you living with Sofia husband and her husband say Sofia not being punish enough. Say she laugh at the fool she make of the guards. Say she gitting along just fine where she at. Happy even, long as she don't have to be no white woman maid.

Gracious God, say Squeak, how I'm gonna tune up my mouth to say all that?

He ast you who you is, make him remember. Tell him how much that quarter he give you meant to you.

That was fifteen years ago, say Squeak, he ain't gonna remember that.

Make him see the Hodges in you, say Odessa. He'll remember.

Tell him you just think justice ought to be done, yourself. But make sure he know you living with Sofia husband, say Shug. Make sure you git in the part bout being happy where she at, worse thing could happen to her is to be some white lady maid.

I don't know, say the prizefighter. This sound mighty much like some ole uncle Tomming to me.

Shug snort, Well, she say, Uncle Tom wasn't call Uncle for nothing.

Dear God,

Poor little Squeak come home with a limp. Her dress rip. Her hat missing and one of the heels come off her shoe.

What happen? us ast.

He saw the Hodges in me, she say. And he didn't like it one bit.

Harpo come up the steps from the car. My wife beat up, my woman rape, he say. I ought to go back out there with guns, maybe set fire to the place, burn the crackers up.

Shut up, Harpo, say Squeak. I'm telling it.

And she do.

Say, the minute I walk through the door, he remembered me.

What he say? us ast.

Say, What you want? I say, I come out of the interest I haves in seeing justice is done. What you say you want? he ast again.

I say what yall told me to say. Bout Sofia not being punish enough. Say she happy in prison, strong girl like her. Her main worry is just the thought of ever being some white woman maid. That what start the fight, you know, I say. Mayor's wife ask Sofia to be her maid. Sofia say she never going to be no white woman's nothing, let alone maid.

That so? he ast, all the time looking me over real good.

Yessir, I say. Say, prison suit her just fine. Shoot, washing and ironing all day is all she do at home. She got six children, you know.

That a fact? he say.

He come from behind his desk, lean over my chair.

Who your folks? he ast.

I tell him my mama's name, grandmama's name. Grandpa's name.

Who your daddy? he ast. Where you git them eyes?

Ain't got no daddy, I say.

Come on now, he say. Ain't I seen you before?

I say, Yessir. And one time bout ten years ago, when I was a little girl, you give me a quarter. I sure did preshate it, I say.

I don't remember that, he say.

You come by the house with my mama friend, Mr Jimmy, I say.

Squeak look round at all of us. Then take a deep breath. Mumble.

Say what? ast Odessa.

Yeah, say Shug, if you can't tell us, who you gon tell, God?

He took my hat off, say Squeak. Told me to undo my dress. She drop her head, put her face in her hands.

My God, say Odessa, and he your uncle.

He say if he was my uncle he wouldn't do it to me. That be a sin. But this just little fornication. Everybody guilty of that.

She turn her face up to Harpo. Harpo, she say, do you really love me, or just my color?

Harpo say, I love you, Squeak. He kneel down and try to put his arms round her waist.

She stand up. My name Mary Agnes, she say.

Dear God,

6 months after Mary Agnes went to git Sofia out of prison, she begin to sing. First she sing Shug's songs, then she begin to make up songs her own self.

She got the kind of voice you never think of trying to sing a song. It little, it high, it sort of meowing. But Mary Agnes don't care.

Pretty soon, us git used to it. Then us like it a whole lot.

Harpo don't know what to make of it.

It seem funny to me, he say to me and Mr ———. So sudden. It put me in the mind of a gramaphone. Sit in the corner a year silent as the grave. Then you put a record on, it come to life.

Wonder if she still mad Sofia knock her teef out? I ast.

Yeah, she mad. But what good being mad gon do? She not evil, she know Sofia life hard to bear right now.

How she git long with the children? ast Mr ———.

They love her, say Harpo. She let 'em do anything they want.

Oh-oh, I say.

Besides, he say, Odessa and Sofia other sisters always on hand to take up the slack. They bring up children like military.

Squeak sing,

They calls me yellow
like yellow be my name

They calls me yellow
like yellow be my name

But if yellow is a name
Why ain't black the same

Well, if I say Hey black girl
Lord, she try to ruin my game

Dear God

Sofia say to me today, I just can't understand it.

What that? I ast.

Why we ain't already kill them off.

Three years after she beat she out of the wash house, got her color and her weight back, look like her old self, just all time think bout killing somebody.

Too many to kill off, I say. Us outnumbered from the start. I speck we knock over one or two, though, here and there, through the years, I say.

We sit on a piece of old crate out near the edge of Miss Millie's yard. Rusty nails stick out long the bottom and when us move they creak gainst the wood.

Sofia job to watch the children play ball. The little boy throw the ball to the little girl, she try to catch it with her eyes shut. It roll up under Sofia foot.

Throw me the ball, say the little boy, with his hands on his hip. Throw me the ball.

Sofia mutter to herself, half to me. I'm here to watch, not to throw, she say. She don't make a move toward the ball.

Don't you hear me talking to you, he shout. He maybe six years old, brown hair, ice blue eyes. He come steaming up to where us sit, haul off and kick Sofia leg. She swing her foot to one side and he scream.

What the trouble? I ast.

Done stab his foot with a rusty nail, Sofia say.

Sure enough, blood come leaking through his shoe.

His little sister come watch him cry. He turn redder and redder. Call his mama.

Miss Millie come running. She scared of Sofia. Everytime she talk to her it like she expect the worst. She don't stand close to her either. When she git a few yards from where us sit, she motion for Billy to come there.

My foot, he say to her.

Sofia do it? she ast.

Little girl pipe up. Billy do it his own self, she say. Trying to kick Sofia leg. The little girl dote on Sofia, always stick up for her. Sofia never notice, she as deef to the little girl as she is to her brother.

Miss Millie cut her eyes at her, put one arm round Billy shoulder and they limp into the back of the house. Little girl follow, wave bye-bye to us.

She seem like a right sweet little thing, I say to Sofia.

Who is? She frown.

The little girl, I say. What they call her, Eleanor Jane?

Yeah, say Sofia, with a real puzzle look on her face, I wonder why she was ever born.

Well, I say, us don't have to wonder that bout darkies.

She giggle. Miss Celie, she say, you just as crazy as you can be.

This the first giggle I heard in three years.

Dear God,

Sofia would make a dog laugh, talking about those people she work for. They have the nerve to try to make us think slavery fell through because of us, say Sofia. Like us didn't have sense enough to handle it. All the time breaking hoe handles and letting the mules loose in the wheat. But how anything they build can last a day is a wonder to me. They backward, she say. Clumsy, and unlucky.

Mayor —— bought Miz Millie a new car, cause she said if colored could have cars then one for her was past due. So he bought her a car, only he refuse to show her how to drive it. Every day he come home from town he look at her, look out the window at her car, say, How you enjoying 'er Miz Millie. She fly off the sofa in a huff, slam the door going in the bathroom.

She ain't got no friends.

So one day she say to me, car been sitting out in the yard two months, Sofia, do you know how to drive? I guess she remembered first seeing me up gainst Buster Broadnax car.

Yes ma'am, I say. I'm slaving away cleaning that big post they got down at the bottom of the stair. They act real funny bout that post. No finger prints is sposed to be on it, ever.

Do you think you could teach me? she says.

One of Sofia children break in, the oldest boy. He tall and handsome, all the time serious. And mad a lot.

He say, Don't say slaving, Mama.

Sofia say, Why not? They got me in a little storeroom up

under the house, hardly bigger than Odessa's porch, and just about as warm in the winter time. I'm at they beck and call all night and all day. They won't let me see my children. They won't let me see no mens. Well, after five years they let me see you once a year. I'm a slave, she say. What would you call it?

A captive, he say.

Sofia go on with her story, only look at him like she glad he hers.

So I say, Yes ma'am. I can teach you, if it the same kind of car I learned on.

Next thing you know there go me and Miz Millie all up and down the road. First I drive and she watch, then she start to try to drive and I watch her. Up and down the road. Soon as I finish cooking breakfast, putting it on the table, washing dishes and sweeping the floor – and just before I go git the mail out of the box down by the road – we go give Miz Millie her driving lesson.

Well, after while she got the hang of it, more or less. Then she really git it. Then one day when we come home from riding, she say to me, I'm gonna drive you home. Just like that.

Home? I ast.

Yes, she say. Home. You ain't been home or seen your children in a while, she say. Ain't that right?

I say, Yes ma'am. It been five years.

She say, That's a shame. You just go git your things right now. Here it is, Christmas. Go get your things. You can stay all day.

For all day I don't need nothing but what I got on, I say.

Fine, she say. Fine. Well git in.

Well, say Sofia, I was so use to sitting up there next to her teaching her how to drive, that I just naturally clammed into the front seat.

She stood outside on her side the car clearing her throat.

Finally she say, Sofia, with a little laugh, This *is* the South.

Yes ma'am, I say.

She clear her throat, laugh some more. Look where you sitting, she say.

I'm sitting where I always sit, I say.

That's the problem, she say. Have you ever seen a white person and a colored sitting side by side in a car, when one of 'em wasn't showing the other one how to drive it or clean it?

I got out the car, opened the back door and clammed in. She sat down up front. Off us traveled down the road, Miz Millie hair blowing all out the window.

It's real pretty country out this way, she say, when we hit the Marshall county road, coming toward Odessa's house.

Yes ma'am, I say.

Then us pull into the yard and all the children come crowding round the car. Nobody told them I was coming, so they don't know who I is. Except the oldest two. They fall on me, and hug me. And then all the little ones start to hug me too. I don't think they even notice I was sitting in the back of the car. Odessa and Jack come out after I was out, so they didn't see it.

Us all stand round kissing and hugging each other, Miz Millie just watching. Finally, she lean out the window and say, Sofia, you only got the rest of the day. I'll be back to pick you up at five o'clock. The children was all pulling me into the house, so sort of over my shoulder I say, Yes ma'am, and I thought I heard her drive off.

But fifteen minutes later, Marion says, That white lady still out there.

Maybe she going to wait to take you back, say Jack.

Maybe she sick, say Odessa. You always say how sickly they is.

I go out to the car, say Sofia, and guess what the matter is? The matter is, she don't know how to do nothing but go forward, and Jack and Odessa's yard too full of trees for that.

Sofia, she say, How you back this thing up?

I lean over the car window and try to show her which way to move the gears. But she flustered and all the children and Odessa and Jack all standing round the porch watching her.

I go round on the other side. Try to explain with my head poked through that window. She stripping gears aplenty by now. Plus her nose red and she look mad and frustrate both.

I clam in the back seat, lean over the back of the front, steady trying to show her how to operate the gears. Nothing happen. Finally the car stop making any sound. Engine dead.

Don't worry, I say, Odessa's husband Jack will drive you home. That's his pick-up right there.

Oh, she say, I couldn't ride in a pick-up with a strange colored man.

I'll ask Odessa to squeeze in too, I say. That would give me a chance to spend a little time with the children, I thought. But she say, No, I don't know her neither.

So it end up with me and Jack driving her back home in the pick-up, then Jack driving me to town to git a mechanic, and at five o'clock I was driving Miz Millie's car back to her house.

I spent fifteen minutes with my children.

And she been going on for months bout how ungrateful I is.

White folks is a miracle of affliction, say Sofia.

Dear God,

Shug write she got a big surprise, and she intend to bring it home for Christmas.

What it is? us wonder.

Mr —— think it a car for him. Shug making big money now, dress in furs all the time. Silk and satin too, and hats made out of gold.

Christmas morning us hear this motor outside the door. Us look out.

Hot diggidy dog, say Mr —— throwing on his pants. He rush to the door. I stand in front the glass trying to make something out my hair. It too short to be long, too long to be short. Too nappy to be kinky, too kinky to be nappy. No set color to it either. I give up, tie on a headrag.

I hear Shug cry, Oh, Albert. He say, *Shug*. I know they hugging. Then I don't hear nothing.

I run out the door. *Shug*, I say, and put out my arms. But before I know anything a skinny big toof man wearing red suspenders is all up in my face. Fore I can wonder whose dog he is, he hugging me.

Miss Celie, he say. Aw, Miss Celie. I heard so much about you. Feel like we old friends.

Shug standing back with a big grin.

This Grady, she say. This my husband.

The minute she say it I know I don't like Grady. I don't like his shape, I don't like his teef, I don't like his clothes. Seem like to me he smell.

Us been driving all night, she say. Nowhere to stop, you know. But here us is. She come over to Grady and put her arms round him, look up at him like he cute and he lean down and give her a kiss.

I glance round at Mr ——. He look like the end of the world. I know I don't look no better.

And this my wedding present to us, say Shug. The car big and dark blue and say Packard on the front. Brand new, she say. She look at Mr ——, take his arm, give it a little squeeze. While we here, Albert, she say, I want you to learn how to drive. She laugh. Grady drive like a fool, she say. I thought the polices was gonna catch us for sure.

Finally Shug really seem to notice me. She come over and hug me a long time. Us two married ladies now, she say. Two married ladies. And hungry, she say. What us got to eat?

Dear God,

Mr —— drink all through Christmas. Him and Grady. Me and Shug cook, talk, clean the house, talk, fix up the tree, talk, wake up in the morning, talk.

She singing all over the country these days. Everybody know her name. She know everybody, too. Know Sophie Tucker, know Duke Ellington, know folks I ain't never heard of. And money. She make so much money she don't know what to do with it. She got a fine house in Memphis, another car. She got one hundred pretty dresses. A room full of shoes. She buy Grady anything he think he want.

Where you find him at? I ast.

Up under my car, she say. The one at home. I drove it after the oil give out, kilt the engine. He the man fixed it. Us took one look at one nother, that was it.

Mr —— feelings hurt, I say. I don't mention mine.

Aw, she say. That old stuff finally over with. You and Albert feel just like family now. Anyhow, once you told me he beat you, and won't work, I felt different about him. If you was my wife, she say, I'd cover you up with kisses stead of licks, and work hard for you too.

He ain't beat me much since you made him quit, I say. Just a slap now and then when he ain't got nothing else to do.

Yall make love any better? she ast.

Us try, I say. He try to play with the button but feel like his fingers dry. Us don't git nowhere much.

You still a virgin? she ast.

I reckon. I say.

◆ 101 ◆

Dear God,

Mr —— and Grady gone off in the car together. Shug ast me could she sleep with me. She cold in her and Grady bed all alone. Us talk bout this and that. Soon talk bout making love. Shug don't actually say making love. She say something nasty. She say fuck.

She ast me, How was it with your children daddy?

The girls had a little separate room, I say, off to itself, connected to the house by a little plank walk. Nobody ever come in there but Mama. But one time when mama not at home, he come. Told me he want me to trim his hair. He bring the scissors and comb and brush and a stool. While I trim his hair he look at me funny. He a little nervous too, but I don't know why, till he grab hold of me and cram me up tween his legs.

I lay there quiet, listening to Shug breathe.

It hurt me, you know, I say. I was just going on fourteen. I never even thought bout men having nothing down there so big. It scare me just to see it. And the way it poke itself and grow.

Shug so quiet I think she sleep.

After he through, I say, he make me finish trimming his hair.

I sneak a look at Shug.

Oh, Miss Celie, she say. And put her arms round me. They black and smooth and kind of glowy from the lamplight.

I start to cry too. I cry and cry and cry. Seem like it all come back to me, laying there in Shug arms. How it hurt and how much I was surprise. How it stung while I finish trimming his hair. How the blood drip down my leg and mess up my stocking. How he don't never look at me straight after that. And Nettie.

Don't cry, Celie, Shug say. Don't cry. She start kissing the water as it come down side my face.

After while I say, Mama finally ast how come she find his hair in the girls room if he don't never go in there like he say. That when he told her I had a boyfriend. Some boy he say he seen sneaking out the back door. It the boy's hair, he say, not his. You know how she love to cut anybody hair, he say.

I did love to cut hair, I say to Shug, since I was a little bitty thing. I'd run go git the scissors if I saw hair coming, and I'd cut and cut, long as I could. That how come I was the one cut his hair. But always before I cut it on the front porch. It got to the place where everytime I saw him coming with the scissors and the comb and the stool, I start to cry.

Shug say, Wellsah, and I thought it was only whitefolks do freakish things like that.

My mama die, I tell Shug. My sister Nettie run away. Mr —— come git me to take care his rotten children. He never ast me nothing bout myself. He clam on top of me and fuck and fuck, even when my head bandaged. Nobody ever love me, I say.

She say, I love you, Miss Celie. And then she haul off and kiss me on the mouth.

Um, she say, like she surprise. I kiss her back, say, *um*, too. Us kiss and kiss till us can't hardly kiss no more. Then us touch each other.

I don't know nothing bout it, I say to Shug.

I don't know much, she say.

Then I feels something real soft and wet on my breast, feel like one of my little lost babies mouth.

Way after while, I act like a little lost baby too.

Dear God,

Grady and Mr —— come staggering in round daybreak. Me and Shug sound asleep. Her back to me, my arms round her waist. What it like? Little like sleeping with mama, only I can't hardly remember ever sleeping with her. Little like sleeping with Nettie, only sleeping with Nettie never feel this good. It warm and cushiony, and I feel Shug's big tits sorta flop over my arms like suds. It feel like heaven is what it feel like, not like sleeping with Mr —— at all.

Wake up Sugar, I say. They back. And Shug roll over, hug me, and git out of the bed. She stagger into the other room and fall on the bed with Grady. Mr —— fall into bed next to me, drunk, and snoring before he hit the quilts.

I try my best to like Grady, even if he do wear red suspenders and bow ties. Even if he do spend Shug's money like he made it himself. Even if he do try to talk like somebody from the North. Memphis, Tennessee ain't North, even I know that. But one thing I sure nuff can't stand, the way he call Shug Mama.

I ain't your fucking mama, Shug say. But he don't pay her no mind.

Like when he be making goo-goo eyes at Squeak and Shug sorta tease him about it, he say, Aw, Mama, you know I don't mean no harm.

Shug like Squeak too, try to help her sing. They sit in Odessa's front room with all the children crowded round them singing and singing. Sometime Swain come with his box, Harpo cook dinner, and me and Mr —— and the prizefighter bring our preshation.

It nice.

Shug say to Squeak, I mean, Mary Agnes, You ought to sing in public.

Mary Agnes say, *Naw*. She think cause she don't sing big and broad like Shug nobody want to hear her. But Shug say she wrong.

What about all them funny voices you hear singing in church? Shug say. What about all them sounds that sound good but they not the sounds you thought folks could make? What bout that? Then she start moaning. Sound like death approaching, angels can't prevent it. It raise the hair on the back of your neck. But it really sound sort of like panthers would sound if they could sing.

I tell you something else, Shug say to Mary Agnes, listening to you sing, folks git to thinking bout a good screw.

Aw, *Miss Shug*, say Mary Agnes, changing color.

Shug say, What, too shamefaced to put singing and dancing and fucking together? She laugh. That's the reason they call what us sing the devil's music. Devils love to fuck. Listen, she say, Let's go sing one night at Harpo place. Be like old times for me. And if I bring you before the crowd, they better listen with respect. Niggers don't know how to act, but if you git through the first half of one song, you got 'em.

You reckon that's the truth? say Mary Agnes. She all big eyed and delight.

I don't know if I want her to sing, say Harpo.

How come? ast Shug. That woman you got singing now can't git her ass *out* the church. Folks don't know whether to dance or creep to the mourner's bench. Plus, you dress Mary Agnes up the right way and you'll make piss pots of money.

Yellow like she is, stringy hair and cloudy eyes, the men'll be crazy bout her. Ain't that right, Grady, she say.

Grady look little sheepish. Grin. Mama you don't miss a thing, he say.

And don't you forgit it, say Shug.

Dear God,

This the letter I been holding in my hand.

Dear Celie,

I know you think I am dead. But I am not. I been writing to you too, over the years, but Albert said you'd never hear from me again and since I never heard from you all this time, I guess he was right. Now I only write at Christmas and Easter hoping my letter get lost among the Christmas and Easter greetings, or that Albert get the holiday spirit and have pity on us.

There is so much to tell you that I don't know, hardly, where to begin — and anyway, you probably won't get this letter, either. I'm sure Albert is still the only one to take mail out of the box.

But if this do get through, one thing I want you to know, I love you, and I am not dead. And Olivia is fine and so is your son.

We are all coming home before the end of another year.

Your loving sister,
Nettie

One night in bed Shug ast me to tell her bout Nettie. What she like? Where she at?

I tell her how Mr —— try to turn her head. How Nettie refuse him, and how he say Nettie have to go.

Where she go? she ast.

I don't know, I say. She leave here.

And no word from her yet? she ast.

Naw, I say. Every day when Mr —— come from the mailbox I hope for news. But nothing come. She dead, I say.

Shug say, She wouldn't be someplace with funny stamps, you don't reckon? She look like she studying. Say, Sometimes when Albert and me walk up to the mailbox there be a letter with a lot of funny looking stamps. He never say nothing bout it, just put it in his inside pocket. One time I ast him could I look at the stamps but he said he'd take it out later. But he never did.

She was just on her way to town, I say. Stamps look like stamps round here. White men with long hair.

Hm, she say, look like a little fat white woman was on one. What your sister Nettie like? she ast. Smart?

Yes, Lord, I say. Smart as anything. Read the newspapers when she was little more than talking. Did figures like they was nothing. Talked real well too. And sweet. There never was a sweeter girl, I say. Eyes just brimming over with it. She love me too, I say to Shug.

She tall or short? Shug ast. What kind of dress she like to wear? What her birthday? What her favorite color? Can she cook? Sew? What about hair?

Everything bout Nettie she want to know.

I talk so much my voice start to go. Why you want to know so much bout Nettie? I ast.

Cause she the only one you ever love, she say, sides me.

Dear God,

All of a sudden Shug buddy-buddy again with Mr ———. They sit on the steps, go down Harpo's. Walk to the mailbox.

Shug laugh and laugh when he got anything to say. Show teef and tits aplenty.

Me and Grady try to carry on like us civilize. But it hard. When I hear Shug laugh I want to choke her, slap Mr ——— face.

All this week I suffer. Grady and me feel so down he turn to reefer, I turn to prayer.

Saturday morning Shug put Nettie letter in my lap. Little fat queen of England stamps on it, plus stamps that got peanuts, coconuts, rubber trees and say Africa. I don't know where England at. Don't know where Africa at either. So I still don't know where Nettie at.

He been keeping your letters, say Shug.

Naw, I say. Mr ——— mean sometimes, but he not that mean.

She say, Humpf, he that mean.

But how come he to do it? I ast. He know Nettie mean everything in the world to me.

Shug say she don't know, but us gon find out.

Us seal the letter up again and put it back in Mr ——— pocket.

He walk round with it in his coat all day. He never mention it. Just talk and laugh with Grady, Harpo and Swain, and try to learn how to drive Shug car.

I watch him so close, I begin to feel a lightening in the head. Fore I know anything I'm standing hind his chair with his razor open.

Then I hear Shug laugh, like something just too funny. She say to me, I know I told you I need something to cut this hangnail with, but Albert git real niggerish bout his razor.

Mr —— look behind him. Put that town, he say. Women, always needing to cut this and shave that, and always gumming up the razor.

Shug got her hand on the razor now. She say, Oh it look dull anyway. She take and sling it back in the shaving box.

All day long I act just like Sofia. I stutter. I mutter to myself. I stumble bout the house crazy for Mr —— blood. In my mind, he falling dead every which a way. By time night come, I can't speak. Every time I open my mouth nothing come out but a little burp.

Shug tell everybody I got a fever and she put me to bed. It probably catching, she say to Mr ——. Maybe you better sleep somewhere else. But she stay with me all night long. I don't sleep. I don't cry. I don't do nothing. I'm cold too. Pretty soon I think maybe I'm dead.

Shug hold me close to her and sometimes talk.

One thing my mama hated me for was how much I love to fuck, she say. She never love to do nothing had anything to do with touching nobody, she say. I try to kiss her, she turn her mouth away. Say, Cut that out Lillie, she say. Lillie Shug's real name. She just so sweet they call her Shug.

My daddy love me to kiss and hug him, but she didn't like the looks of that. So when I met Albert, and once I got in his arms, nothing could git me out. It was good, too, she say. You know for me to have three babies by Albert and Albert weak as he is, it had to be good.

I had every one of my babies at home, too. Midwife come, preacher come, a bunch of the good ladies from the church.

Just when I hurt so much I don't know my own name, they think a good time to talk bout repent.

She laugh. I was too big a fool to repent. Then she say, I loved me some Albert ———.

I don't even want to say nothing. Where I'm at it peaceful. It calm. No Albert there. No Shug. Nothing.

Shug say, the last baby did it. They turned me out. I went to stay with my mama wild sister in Memphis. She just like me, Mama say. She drink, she fight, she love mens to death. She work in a roadhouse. Cook. Feed fifty men, screw fifty-five.

Shug talk and talk.

And dance, she say. Nobody dance like Albert when he was young. Sometime us did the moochie for a hour. After that, nothing to do but go somewhere and lay down. And funny. Albert was so *funny*. He kept me laughing. How come he ain't funny no more? she ast. How come he never hardly laugh? How come he don't dance? she say. Good God, Celie, she say, What happen to the man I love?

She quiet a little while. Then she say, I was so surprise when I heard he was going to marry Annie Julia, she say. Too surprise to be hurt. I didn't believe it. After all, Albert knew as well as me that love would have to go some to be better than ours. Us had the kind of love couldn't be improve. That's what I thought.

But, he weak, she say. His daddy told him I'm trash, my mama trash before me. His brother say the same. Albert try to stand up for us, git knock down. One reason they give him for not marrying me is cause I have children.

But they *his*, I told old Mr ———.

How us know? He ast.

Poor Annie Julia, Shug say. She never had a chance. I was so mean, and so wild, Lord. I used to go round saying, I don't care who he married to, I'm gonna fuck him. She stop talking a minute. Then she say, And I did, too. Us fuck so much in the open us give fucking a bad name.

But he fuck Annie Julia too, she say, and she didn't have nothing, not even a liking for him. Her family forgot about her once she married. And then Harpo and all the children start to come. Finally she start to sleep with that man that shot her down. Albert beat her. The children dragged on her. Sometimes I wonder what she thought about while she died.

I know what I'm thinking bout, I think. Nothing. And as much of it as I can.

I went to school with Annie Julia, Shug say. She was pretty, man. Black as anything, and skin just as smooth. Big black eyes look like moons. And sweet too. Hell, say Shug, I liked her myself. Why I hurt her so? I used to keep Albert away from home for a week at a time. She'd come and beg him for money to buy groceries for the children.

I feel a few drops of water on my hand.

And when I come here, say Shug. I treated you so mean. Like you was a servant. And all because Albert married you. And I didn't even want him for a husband, she say. I never really wanted Albert for a husband. But just to choose me, you know, cause nature had already done it. Nature said, You two folks, hook up, cause you a good example of how it sposed to go. I didn't want nothing to be able to go against that. But what was good tween us must have been nothing but bodies, she say. Cause I don't know the Albert that don't dance, can't hardly laugh, never talk bout nothing, beat you and hid your sister Nettie's letters. Who he?

I don't know nothing, I think. And glad of it.

Dear God,

Now that I know Albert hiding Nettie's letters, I know exactly where they is. They in his trunk. Everything that mean something to Albert go in his trunk. He keep it locked up tight, but Shug can git the key.

One night when Mr —— and Grady gone, us open the trunk. Us find a lot of Shug's underclothes, some nasty picture postcards, and way down under his tobacco, Nettie's letters. Bunches and bunches of them. Some fat, some thin. Some open, some not.

How us gon do this? I ast Shug.

She say, Simple. We take the letters out of the envelopes, leave the envelopes just like they is. I don't think he look in this corner of the trunk much, she say.

I heated the stove, put on the kettle. Us steam and steam the envelopes until we had all the letters laying on the table. Then us put the envelopes back inside the trunk.

I'm gonna put them in some kind of order for you, say Shug.

Yeah, I say, but don't let's do it in here, let's go in you and Grady room.

So she got up and us went into they little room. Shug sat in a chair by the bed with all Nettie letters spread round her, I got on the bed with the pillows behind my back.

These the first ones, say Shug. They postmark right here.

Dear Celie, *the first letter say,*

You've got to fight and get away from Albert. He ain't no good.

When I left you all's house, walking, he followed me on his horse. When we was well out of sight of the house he caught up with me and started trying to talk. You know how he do, You sure is looking fine, Miss Nettie, and stuff like that. I tried to ignore him and walk faster, but my bundles was heavy and the sun was hot. After while I had to rest, and that's when he got down from his horse and started to try to kiss me, and drag me back in the woods.

Well, I started to fight him, and with God's help, I hurt him bad enough to make him let me alone. But he was some mad. He said because of what I'd done I'd never hear from you again, and you would never hear from me.

I was so mad myself I was shaking.

Anyhow, I got a ride into town on somebody's wagon. And that same somebody pointed me in the direction of the Reverend Mr ———'s place. And what was my surprise when a little girl opened the door and she had your eyes set in your face.

love,
Nettie

Next one said,

Dear Celie,

I keep thinking it's too soon to look for a letter from you. And I know how busy you is with all Mr ——'s children. But I miss you *so* much. Please write to me, soon as you have a chance. Every day I think about you. Every minute.

The lady you met in town is name Corrine. The little girl's name is Olivia. The husband's name is Samuel. The little boy's name is Adam. They are sanctified religious and very good to me. They live in a nice house next to the church where Samuel preaches, and we spend a lot of time on church business. I say 'we' because they always try to include me in everything they do, so I don't feel so left out and alone.

But God, I miss you, Celie. I think about the time you laid yourself down for me. I love you with all my heart,

Your sister,

Nettie

Next one say,

Dearest Celie,

By now I am almost crazy. I think Albert told me the truth, and that he is not giving you my letters. The only person I can think of who could help us out is Pa, but I don't want him to know where I am.

I asked Samuel if he would visit you and Mr ———, just to see how you are. But he says he can't risk putting himself between man and wife, especially when he don't know them. And I felt bad for having to ask him, he and Corrine have been so nice to me. But my heart is breaking. It is breaking because I can not find any work in this town, and I will have to leave. After I leave, what will happen to us? How will we ever know what is going on?

Corrine and Samuel and the children are part of a group of people called Missionaries, of the American and African Missionary Society. They have ministered to the Indians out west and are ministering to the poor of this town. All in preparation for the work they feel they were born for, missionary work in Africa.

I dread parting from them because in the short time we've been together they've been like family to me. Like family might have been, I mean.

Write if you can. Here are some stamps.

love, Nettie

Next one, fat, dated two months later, say,

Dear Celie,

I wrote a letter to you almost every day on the ship coming to Africa. But by the time we docked I was so down, I tore them into little pieces and dropped them into the water. Albert is not going to let you have my letters and so what use is there in writing them. That's the way I felt when I tore them up and sent them to you on the waves. But now I feel different.

I remember one time you said your life made you feel so ashamed you couldn't even talk about it to God, you had to write it, bad as you thought your writing was. Well, now I know what you meant. And whether God will read letters or no, I know you will go on writing them; which is guidance enough for me. Anyway, when I don't write to you I feel as bad as I do when I don't pray, locked up in myself and choking on my own heart. I am so *lonely*, Celie.

The reason I am in Africa is because one of the missionaries that was supposed to go with Corrine and Samuel to help with the children and with setting up a school suddenly married a man who was afraid to let her go, and refused to come to Africa with her. So there they were, all set to go, with a ticket suddenly available and no missionary to give it to. At the same time, I wasn't able to find a job anywhere around town. But I never dreamed of going to Africa! I never even thought about it as a real place, though Samuel and Corrine and even the children talked about it all the time.

Miss Beasley used to say it was a place overrun with savages who didn't wear clothes. Even Corrine and Samuel thought like this at times. But they know a lot more about it than Miss Beasley or any of our other teachers, and besides, they spoke of all the good things they could do for the downtrodden people from whom they sprang. People who need Christ and good medical advice.

One day I was in town with Corrine and we saw the mayor's wife and her maid. The mayor's wife was shopping – going in and out of stores – and her maid was waiting for her on the street and taking the packages. I don't know if you have ever seen the mayor's wife. She looks like a wet cat. And there was her maid looking like the very last person in the world you'd expect to see waiting on anybody, and in particular not on anybody that looked like that.

I spoke. But just speaking to me seemed to make her embarrassed and she suddenly sort of erased herself. It was the strangest thing, Celie! One minute I was saying howdy to a living woman. The next minute nothing living was there. Only its shape.

All that night I thought about it. Then Samuel and Corrine told me what they'd heard about how she got to be the mayor's maid. That she attacked the mayor, and then the mayor and his wife took her from the prison to work in their home.

In the morning I started asking questions about Africa and started reading all the books Samuel and Corrine have on the subject.

Did you know there were great cities in Africa, greater than Milledgeville or even Atlanta, thousands of years ago? That the Egyptians who built the pyramids and enslaved the Israelites were colored? That Egypt is in Africa? That the Ethiopia we read about in the bible meant all of Africa?

Well, I read and I read until I thought my eyes would fall

out. I read where the Africans sold us because they loved money more than their own sisters and brothers. How we came to America in ships. How we were made to work.

I hadn't realized I was so *ignorant*, Celie. The little I knew about my own self wouldn't have filled a thimble! And to think Miss Beasley always said I was the smartest child she ever taught! But one thing I do thank her for, for teaching me to learn for myself, by reading and studying and writing a clear hand. And for keeping alive in me somehow the desire to *know*. So when Corrine and Samuel asked me if I would come with them and help them build a school in the middle of Africa, I said yes. But only if they would teach me everything they knew to make me useful as a missionary and someone they would not be ashamed to call a friend. They agreed to this condition, and my real education began at that time.

They have been as good as their word. And I study everything night and day.

Oh, Celie, there are colored people in the world who want us to know! Want us to grow and see the light! They are not all mean like Pa and Albert, or beaten down like ma was. Corrine and Samuel have a wonderful marriage. Their only sorrow in the beginning was that they could not have children. And then, they say, 'God' sent them Olivia and Adam.

I wanted to say, 'God' has sent you their sister and aunt, but I didn't. Yes, their children, sent by 'God' are your children, Celie. And they are being brought up in love, Christian charity and awareness of God. And now 'God' has sent me to watch over them, to protect and cherish them. To lavish all the love I feel for you on them. It is a miracle, isn't it? And no doubt impossible for you to believe.

But on the other hand, if you can believe I am in Africa, and I am, you can believe anything.

Your sister, Nettie

The next letter after that one say,

Dear Celie,

While we were in town Corrine bought cloth to make me two sets of traveling outfits. One olive green and the other gray. Long gored skirts and suit jackets to be worn with white cotton blouses and lace-up boots. She also bought me a woman's boater with a checkered band.

Although I work for Corrine and Samuel and look after the children, I don't feel like a maid. I guess this is because they teach me, and I teach the children and there's no beginning or end to teaching and learning and working – it all runs together.

Saying goodbye to our church group was hard. But happy, too. Everyone has such high hopes for what can be done in Africa. Over the pulpit there is a saying: *Ethiopia Shall Stretch Forth Her Hands to God.* Think what it means that Ethiopia is Africa! All the Ethiopians in the bible were colored. It had never occurred to me, though when you read the bible it is perfectly plain if you pay attention only to the words. It is the pictures in the bible that fool you. The pictures that illustrate the words. All of the people are white and so you just think all the people from the bible were white too. But really *white* white people lived somewhere else during those times. That's why the bible says that Jesus Christ had hair like lamb's wool. Lamb's wool is not straight, Celie. It isn't even curly.

What can I tell you about New York – or even about the train that took us there! We had to ride in the sit-down section of the train, but Celie, there are beds on trains! And a restaurant! And toilets! The beds come down out of the walls, over the tops of the seats, and are called berths. Only white people can ride in the beds and use the restaurant. And they have different toilets from colored.

One white man on the platform in South Carolina asked us where we were going – we had got off the train to get some fresh air and to dust the grit and dust out of our clothes. When we said Africa he looked offended and tickled too. Niggers going to Africa, he said to his wife. Now I *have* seen everything.

When we got to New York we were tired and dirty. But so excited! Listen, Celie, New York is a *beautiful* city. And colored own a whole section of it, called Harlem. There are colored people in more fancy motor cars than I thought existed, and living in houses that are finer than any white person's house down home. There are more than a hundred churches! And we went to every one of them. And I stood before each congregation with Samuel and Corrine and the children and sometimes our mouths just dropped open from the generosity and goodness of those Harlem people's hearts. They live in such beauty and dignity, Celie. And they give and give and then reach down and give some more, when the name 'Africa' is mentioned.

They *love* Africa. They defend it at the drop of a hat. And speaking of hats, if we had passed our hats alone they would not have been enough to hold all the donations to our enterprise. Even the children dredged up their pennies. Please give these to the children of Africa, they said. They were all dressed so beautifully, too, Celie. I wish you could have seen them. There is a fashion in Harlem now for boys to wear something called knickers – sort of baggy pants, fitted tight just below the knee, and for girls to wear garlands of flowers in their hair. They must be the most beautiful children alive, and Adam and Olivia couldn't take their eyes off them.

Then there were the dinners we were invited to, the

breakfasts, lunches, and suppers. I gained five pounds just from tasting. I was too excited to really eat.

And all the people have indoor toilets, Celie. And gas or electric lights!

Well, we had two weeks of study in the Olinka dialect, which the people in this region speak. Then we were examined by a doctor (colored!) and given medical supplies for ourselves and for our host village by the Missionary Society of New York. It is run by white people and they didn't say anything about caring about Africa, but only about duty. There is already a white woman missionary not far from our village who has lived in Africa for the past twenty years. She is said to be much loved by the natives even though she thinks they are an entirely different species from what she calls Europeans. Europeans are white people who live in a place called Europe. That is where the white people down home came from. She says an African daisy and an English daisy are both flowers, but totally different kinds. The man at the Society says she is successful because she doesn't 'coddle' her charges. She also speaks their language. He is a white man who looks at us as if we cannot possibly be as good with the Africans as this woman is.

My spirits sort of drooped after being at the Society. On every wall there was a picture of a white man. Somebody called Speke, somebody called Livingstone. Somebody called Daly. Or was it Stanley? I looked for a picture of the white woman but didn't see one. Samuel looked a little sad too, but then he perked up and reminded us that there is one big advantage we have. We are not white. We are not Europeans. We are black like the Africans themselves. And that we and the Africans will be working for a common goal: the uplift of black people everywhere.

Your sister, Nettie

Dear Celie,

Samuel is a big man. He dresses in black almost all the time, except for his white clerical collar. And *he* is black. Until you see his eyes you think he's somber, even mean, but he has the most thoughtful and gentle brown eyes. When he says something it settles you, because he never says anything off the top of his head and he's never out to dampen your spirit or to hurt. Corrine is a lucky woman to have him as her husband.

But let me tell you about the ship! The ship, called *The Malaga*, was three stories high! And we had rooms (called cabins) with beds. Oh, Celie, to lie in a bed in the middle of the ocean! And the ocean! Celie, more water than you can imagine in one place. It took us two weeks to cross it! And then we were in England, which is a country full of white people and some of them very nice and with their own Anti-Slavery & Missionary Society. The churches in England were also very eager to help us and white men and women, who looked just like the ones at home, invited us to their gatherings and into their homes for tea, and to talk about our work. 'Tea' to the English is really a picnic indoors. Plenty of sandwiches and cookies and of course hot tea. We all used the same cups and plates.

Everyone said I seemed very young to be a missionary, but Samuel said that I was very willing, and that, anyway, my primary duties would be helping with the children and teaching a kindergarten class or two.

Our work began to seem somewhat clearer in England because the English have been sending missionaries to Africa and India and China and God knows where all, for over a hundred years. And the things they have brought back! We spent a morning in one of their museums and it was packed with jewels, furniture, fur carpets, swords, clothing, even *tombs* from all the countries they have been. From Africa they have *thousands* of vases, jars, masks, bowls, baskets, statues – and they are all so beautiful it is hard to imagine that the people who made them don't still exist. And yet the English assure us they do not. Although Africans once had a better civilization than the European (though of course even the English do not say this: I get this from reading a man named J. A. Rogers) for several centuries they have fallen on hard times. 'Hard times' is a phrase the English love to use, when speaking of Africa. And it is easy to forget that Africa's 'hard times' were made harder by them. Millions and millions of Africans were captured and sold into slavery – you and me, Celie! And whole cities were destroyed by slave catching wars. Today the people of Africa – having murdered or sold into slavery their strongest folks – are riddled by disease and sunk in spiritual and physical confusion. They believe in the devil and worship the dead. Nor can they read or write.

Why did they sell us? How could they have done it? And why do we still love them? These were the thoughts I had as we tramped through the chilly streets of London. I studied England on a map, so neat and serene, and I became hopeful in spite of myself that much good for Africa is possible, given hard work and the right frame of mind. And then we sailed for Africa. Leaving Southampton, England on the 24th of July and arriving in Monrovia, Liberia on the 12th of September. On the way we stopped in Lisbon, Portugal and Dakar, Senegal.

Monrovia was the last place we were among people we

were somewhat used to, since it is an African country that was 'founded' by ex-slaves from America who came back to Africa to live. Had any of their parents or grandparents been sold *from* Monrovia, I wondered, and what was their feeling, once sold as slaves, now coming back, with close ties to the country that bought them, to rule.

Celie, I must stop now. The sun is not so hot now and I must prepare for the afternoon classes and vesper service.

I wish you were with me, or I with you.

My love,

Your sister, Nettie

Dearest Celie,

It was the funniest thing to stop over in Monrovia after my first glimpse of Africa, which was Senegal. The capital of Senegal is Dakar and the people speak their own language, Senegalese I guess they would call it, and French. They are the blackest people I have ever seen, Celie. They are black like the people we are talking about when we say, 'So and so is blacker than black, he's *blue*black.' They are so black, Celie, they shine. Which is something else folks down home like to say about real black folks. But Celie, try to imagine a city full of these shining, blueblack people wearing brilliant blue robes with designs like fancy quilt patterns. Tall, thin, with long necks and straight backs. Can you picture it at all, Celie? Because I felt like I was seeing black for the first time. And Celie, there is something magical about it. Because the black is so black the eye is simply dazzled, and then there is the shining that seems to come, really, from moonlight, it is so luminous, but their skin glows even in the sun.

But I did not really like the Senegalese I met in the market. They were concerned only with their sale of produce. If we did not buy, they looked through us as quickly as they looked through the white French people who live there. Somehow I had not expected to see any white people in Africa, but they are here in droves. And not all are missionaries.

There are bunches of them in Monrovia, too. And the president, whose last name is Tubman, has some in his cabinet. He also has a lot of white-looking colored men in his cabinet. On our second evening in Monrovia we had tea at the presidential palace. It looks very much like the American white house (where our president lives) Samuel says. The president talked a good bit about his efforts trying to develop the country and about his problems with the natives, who don't want to work to help build the country up. It was the first time I'd heard a black man use that word. I knew that to white people all colored people are natives. But he cleared his throat and said he only meant 'native' to Liberia. I did not see any of these 'natives' in his cabinet. And none of the cabinet members' wives could pass for natives. Compared to them in their silks and pearls, Corrine and I were barely dressed, let alone dressed for the occasion. But I think the women we saw at the palace spend a lot of their time dressing. Still, they look dissatisfied. Not like the cheery schoolteachers we saw only by chance, as they herded their classes down to the beach for a swim.

Before we left we visited one of the large cacoa plantations they have. Nothing but cacoa trees as far as the eye can see. And whole villages built right in the middle of the fields. We watched the weary families come home from work, still carrying their cacoa seed buckets in their hands (these double as lunch buckets next day), and sometimes – if they are women – their children on their backs. As tired as they are, they sing! Celie. Just like we do at home. Why do tired people sing? I asked Corrine. Too tired to do anything else, she said. Besides, they don't own the cacoa fields, Celie, even president Tubman doesn't own them. People in a place called Holland do. The people who make Dutch chocolate. And there are overseers who make sure the people work hard, who live in stone houses in the corners of the fields.

Again I must go. Everyone is in bed and I am writing by lamplight. But the light is attracting so many bugs I am being eaten alive. I have bites everywhere, including my scalp and the bottoms of my feet.

But —

Did I mention my first sight of the African coast? Something struck in me, in my soul, Celie, like a large bell, and I just vibrated. Corrine and Samuel felt the same. And we kneeled down right on deck and gave thanks to God for letting us see the land for which our mothers and fathers cried — and lived and died — to see again.

Oh, Celie! Will I ever be able to tell you all?

I dare not ask, I know. But leave it all to God.

Your everloving sister, Nettie

Dear God,

What with being shock, crying and blowing my nose, and trying to puzzle out words us don't know, it took a long time to read just the first two or three letters. By the time us got up to where she good and settled in Africa, Mr —— and Grady come home.

Can you handle it? ast Shug.

How I'm gon keep from killing him, I say.

Don't kill, she say. Nettie be coming home before long. Don't make her have to look at you like us look at Sofia.

But it so hard, I say, while Shug empty her suitcase and put the letters inside.

Hard to be Christ too, say Shug. But he manage. Remember that. Thou Shalt Not Kill, He said. And probably wanted to add on to that, Starting with me. He knowed the fools he was dealing with.

But Mr —— not Christ. I'm not Christ, I say.

You somebody to Nettie, she say. And she be pissed if you change on her while she on her way home.

Us hear Grady and Mr —— in the kitchen. Dishes rattling, safe door open and shut.

Naw, I think I feel better if I kill him, I say. I feels sickish. Numb, now.

Naw you won't. Nobody feel better for killing nothing. They feel *something* is all.

That better than nothing.

Celie, she say, Nettie not the only one you got to worry bout.

Say what? I ast.

Me, Celie, think about me a little bit. Miss Celie, if you kill Albert, Grady be all I got left. I can't even stand the thought of that.

I laugh, thinking bout Grady's big toofs.

Make Albert let me sleep with you from now on, while you here, I say.

And somehow or other, she do.

Dear God,

Us sleep like sisters, me and Shug. Much as I still want to be with her, much as I love to look, my titties stay soft, my little button never rise. Now I know I'm dead. But she say, Naw, just being mad, grief, wanting to kill somebody will make you feel this way. Nothing to worry about. Titties gonna perk up, button gonna rise again.

I loves to hug up, period, she say. Snuggle. Don't need nothing else right now.

Yeah, I say. Hugging is good. Snuggle. All of it's good.

She say, Times like this, lulls, us ought to do something different.

Like what? I ast.

Well, she say, looking me up and down, let's make you some pants.

What I need pants for? I say. I ain't no man.

Don't git uppity, she say. But you don't have a dress do nothing for you. You not made like no dress pattern, neither.

I don't know, I say. Mr —— not going to let his wife wear pants.

Why not? say Shug. You do all the work around here. It's a scandless, the way you look out there plowing in a dress. How you keep from falling over it or getting the plow caught in it is beyond me.

Yeah? I say.

Yeah. And another thing, I used to put on Albert's pants when we was courting. And he one time put on my dress.

No he didn't.

Yes he did. He use to be a lot of fun. Not like now. But he loved to see me in pants. It was like a red flag to a bull.

Ugh, I say. I could just picture it, and I didn't like it one bit.

Well, you know how they is, say Shug.

What us gon make 'em out of, I say.

We have to git our hands on somebody's army uniform, say Shug. For practice. That good strong material and free.

Jack, I say. Odessa's husband.

Okay, she say. And every day we going to read Nettie's letters and sew.

A needle and not a razor in my hand, I think.

She don't say nothing else, just come over to me and hug.

Dear God,

Now I know Nettie alive I begin to strut a little bit. Think,
When she come home us leave here. Her and me and our two
children. What they look like, I wonder. But it hard to think
bout them. I feels shame. More than love, to tell the truth.
Anyway, is they all right here? Got good sense and all? Shug
say children got by incest turn into dunces. Incest part of the
devil's plan.

But I think bout Nettie.

It's hot, here, Celie, she write. Hotter than July. Hotter
than August *and* July. Hot like cooking dinner on a big stove
in a little kitchen in August and July. Hot.

Dear Celie,

We were met at the ship by an African from the village we
are settling in. His Christian name is Joseph. He is short and
fat, with hands that seem not to have any bones in them.
When he shook my hand it felt like something soft and damp
was falling and I almost caught it. He speaks a little English,
what they call pidgin English. It is very different from the
way we speak English, but somehow familiar. He helped us
unload our things from the ship into the boats that came out
to get us. These boats are really dug-out canoes, like the
Indians had, the ones you see in pictures. With all our
belongings we filled three of them, and a fourth one carried
our medical and teaching supplies.

Once in the boat we were entertained by the songs of our

boatmen as they tried to outpaddle each other to the shore. They paid very little attention to us or our cargo. When we reached the shore they didn't bother to help us alight from the boat and actually set some of our supplies right down in the water. As soon as they had browbeat poor Samuel out of a tip that Joseph said was too big, they were off hallooing another group of people who were waiting at the edge of the water to be taken to the ship.

The port is pretty, but too shallow for large ships to use. So there is a good business for the boatmen, during the season the ships come by. These boatmen were all considerably larger and more muscular than Joseph, though all of them, including Joseph, are a deep chocolate brown. Not black, like the Senegalese. And Celie, they all have the strongest, cleanest, whitest teeth! I was thinking about teeth a lot on the voyage over, because I had toothache nearly the entire time. You know how rotten my back teeth are. And in England I was struck by the English people's teeth. So crooked, usually, and blackish with decay. I wondered if it was the English water. But the Africans' teeth remind me of horses' teeth, they are so fully formed, straight and strong.

The port's 'town' is the size of the hardware store in town. Inside there are stalls filled with cloth, hurricane lamps and oil, mosquito netting, camp bedding, hammocks, axes and hoes and machetes and other tools. The whole place is run by a white man, but some of the stalls that sell produce are rented out to Africans. Joseph showed us things we needed to buy. A large iron pot for boiling water and our clothes, a zinc basin. Mosquito netting. Nails. Hammer and saw and pick-ax. Oil and lamps.

Since there was nowhere to sleep in the port, Joseph hired some porters from among the young men loafing around the trading post and we left right away for Olinka, some four days march through the bush. Jungle, to you. Or maybe not.

Do you know what a jungle is? Well. Trees and trees and then more trees on top of that. And big. They are so big they look like they were built. And vines. And ferns. And little animals. Frogs. Snakes too, according to Joseph. But thank God we did not see any of these, only humpbacked lizards as big as your arm which the people here catch and eat.

They love meat. All the people in this village. Sometimes if you can't get them to do anything any other way, you start to mention meat, either a little piece extra you just happen to have or maybe, if you want them to do something big, you talk about a barbecue. Yes, a barbecue. They remind me of folks at home!

Well, we got here. And I thought I would never get the kinks out of my hips from being carried in a hammock the whole way. Everybody in the village crowded round us. Coming out of little round huts with something that I thought was straw on top of them but is really a kind of leaf that grows everywhere. They pick it and dry it and lay it so it overlaps to make the roof rainproof. This part is women's work. Menfolks drive the stakes for the hut and sometimes help build the walls with mud and rock from the streams.

You never saw such curious faces as the village folks surrounded us with. At first they just looked. Then one or two of the women touched my and Corrine's dresses. My dress was so dirty round the hem from dragging on the ground for three nights of cooking round a campfire that I was ashamed of myself. But then I took a look at the dresses they were wearing. Most looked like they'd been drug across the yard by the pigs. And they don't fit. So then they moved up a little bit – nobody saying a word yet – and touched our hair. Then looked down at our shoes. We looked at Joseph. Then he told us they were acting this way because the missionaries before us were all white. And they naturally thought all missionaries were white people, and vice versa.

The men had been to the port, some of them, and had seen the white merchant, so they knew white men could be something else too. But the women had never been to the port and the only white person they'd seen was the missionary they had buried a year ago.

Samuel asked if they'd ever seen the white woman missionary twenty miles further on, and he said no. Twenty miles through the jungle is a very long trip. The men might hunt up to ten miles around the village, but the women stayed close to their huts and fields.

Then one of the women asked a question. We looked at Joseph. He said the woman wanted to know if the children belonged to me or to Corrine or to both of us. Joseph said they belonged to Corrine. The woman looked us both over, and said something else. We looked at Joseph. He said the woman said they both looked like me. We all laughed politely.

Then another woman had a question. She wanted to know if I was also Samuel's wife.

Joseph said no, that I was a missionary just like Samuel and Corrine. Then someone said they never suspected missionaries could have children. Then another said he never dreamed missionaries could be black.

Then someone said, That the new missionaries would be black and two of them women was exactly what he *had* dreamed, and just last night, too.

By now there was a lot of commotion. Little heads began to pop from behind mothers' skirts and over big sisters' shoulders. And we were sort of swept along among the villagers, about three hundred of them, to a place without walls but with a leaf roof, where we all sat down on the ground, men in front, women and children behind. Then there was loud whispering among some very old men who looked like the church elders back home – with their baggy trousers and shiny, ill-fitting coats – Did black missionaries drink palm wine?

Corrine looked at Samuel and Samuel looked at Corrine. But me and the children were already drinking it, because someone had already put the little brown clay glasses in our hands and we were too nervous not to start sipping.

We got there around four o'clock, and sat under the leaf canopy until nine. We had our first meal there, a chicken and groundnut (peanut) stew which we ate with our fingers. But mostly we listened to songs and watched dances that raised lots of dust.

The biggest part of the welcoming ceremony was about the roofleaf, which Joseph interpreted for us as one of the villagers recited the story that it is based upon. The people of this village think they have always lived on the exact spot where their village now stands. And this spot has been good to them. They plant cassava fields that yield huge crops. They plant groundnuts that do the same. They plant yam and cotton and millet. All kinds of things. But once, a long time ago, one man in the village wanted more than his share of land to plant. He wanted to make more crops so as to use his surplus for trade with the white men on the coast. Because he was chief at the time, he gradually took more and more of the common land, and took more and more wives to work it. As his greed increased he also began to cultivate the land on which the roofleaf grew. Even his wives were upset by this and tried to complain, but they were lazy women and no one paid any attention to them. Nobody could remember a time when roofleaf did not exist in overabundant amounts. But eventually, the greedy chief took so much of this land that even the elders were disturbed. So he simply bought them off – with axes and cloth and cooking pots that he got from the coast traders.

But then there came a great storm during the rainy season that destroyed all the roofs on all the huts in the village, and the people discovered to their dismay that there was no longer any roofleaf to be found. Where roofleaf had flourished from time's beginning, there was cassava. Millet. Groundnuts.

For six months the heavens and the winds abused the people of Olinka. Rain came down in spears, stabbing away the mud of their walls. The wind was so fierce it blew the rocks out of the walls and into the people's cooking pots. Then cold rocks, shaped like millet balls, fell from the sky, striking everyone, men and women and children alike, and giving them fevers. The children fell ill first, then their parents. Soon the village began to die. By the end of the rainy season, half the village was gone.

The people prayed to their gods and waited impatiently for the seasons to change. As soon as the rain stopped they rushed to the old roofleaf beds and tried to find the old roots. But of the endless numbers that had always grown there, only a few dozen remained. It was five years before the roof-leaf became plentiful again. During those five years many more in the village died. Many left, never to return. Many were eaten by animals. Many, many were sick. The chief was given all his storebought utensils and forced to walk away from the village forever. His wives were given to other men.

On the day when all the huts had roofs again from the roofleaf, the villagers celebrated by singing and dancing and telling the story of the roofleaf. The roofleaf became the thing they worship.

Looking over the heads of the children at the end of this tale, I saw coming slowly towards us, a large brown spiky thing as big as a room, with a dozen legs walking slowly and carefully under it. When it reached our canopy, it was presented to us. It was our roof.

As it approached, the people bowed down.

The white missionary before you would not let us have this ceremony, said Joseph. But the Olinka like it very much.

We know a roofleaf is not Jesus Christ, but in its own humble way, is it not God?

So there we sat, Celie, face to face with the Olinka God. And Celie, I was so tired and sleepy and full of chicken and groundnut stew, my ears ringing with song, that all that Joseph said made perfect sense to me.

I wonder what you will make of all this?

I send my love,

Your sister,
Nettie

Dear Celie,

It has been a long time since I had time to write. But always, no matter what I'm doing, I am writing to you. Dear Celie, I say in my head in the middle of Vespers, the middle of the night, while cooking, Dear, dear Celie. And I imagine that you really do get my letters and that you are writing me back: Dear Nettie, this is what life is like for me.

We are up at five o'clock for a light breakfast of millet porridge and fruit, and the morning classes. We teach the children English, reading, writing, history, geography, arithmetic and the stories of the bible. At eleven o'clock we break for lunch and household duties. From one until four it is too hot to move, though some of the mothers sit behind their huts and sew. At four o'clock we teach the older children and at night we are available for adults. Some of the older children are used to coming to the mission school, but the smaller ones are not. Their mothers sometimes drag them here, screaming and kicking. They are all boys. Olivia is the only girl.

The Olinka do not believe girls should be educated. When I asked a mother why she thought this, she said: A girl is nothing to herself; only to her husband can she become something.

What can she become? I asked.

Why, she said, the mother of his children.

But I am not the mother of anybody's children, I said, and I am something.

You are not much, she said. The missionary's drudge.

It is true that I work harder here than I ever dreamed I could work, and that I sweep out the school and tidy up after service, but I don't feel like a drudge. I was surprised that this woman, whose Christian name is Catherine, saw me in this light.

She has a little girl, Tashi, who plays with Olivia after school. Adam is the only boy who will speak to Olivia at school. They are not mean to her, it is just — what is it? Because she is where they are doing 'boys' things' they do not see her. But never fear, Celie, Olivia has your stubbornness and clear-sightedness, and she is smarter than all of them, including Adam, put together.

Why can't Tashi come to school? she asked me. When I told her the Olinka don't believe in educating girls she said, quick as a flash, They're like white people at home who don't want colored people to learn.

Oh, she's sharp, Celie. At the end of the day, when Tashi can get away from all the chores her mother assigns her, she and Olivia secret themselves in my hut and everything Olivia has learned she shares with Tashi. To Olivia right now Tashi alone is Africa. The Africa she came beaming across the ocean hoping to find. Everything else is difficult for her.

The insects, for instance. For some reason, all of her bites turn into deep, runny sores, and she has a lot of trouble sleeping at night because the noises from the forest frighten her. It is taking a long time for her to become used to the food, which is nourishing but, for the most part, indifferently prepared. The women of the village take turns cooking for us, and some are cleaner and more conscientious than others. Olivia gets sick from the food prepared by any of the chiefs wives. Samuel thinks it may be the water they use, which comes from a separate spring that runs clear even in the dry season. But the rest of us have no ill effects. It is as if Olivia fears the food from these wives because they all look so unhappy and work so hard. Whenever they see her they talk about the day when she will become their littlest sister/wife. It is just a joke, and they like her, but I wish they wouldn't say it. Even though they are unhappy and work like donkeys they still think it is an honor to be the chiefs wife. He walks around all day holding his belly up and talking and drinking palm wine with the healer.

Why do they say I will be a wife of the chief? asks Olivia.

That is as high as they can think, I tell her.

He is fat and shiny with huge perfect teeth. She thinks she has nightmares about him.

You will grow up to be a strong Christian woman, I tell her. Someone who helps her people to advance. You will be a teacher or a nurse. You will travel. You will know many people greater than the chief.

Will Tashi? she wants to know.

Yes, I tell her, Tashi too.

Corrine said to me this morning, Nettie, to stop any kind of confusion in the minds of these people, I think we should call one another brother and sister, all the time. Some of them can't seem to get it through their thick skulls that you are not Samuel's other wife. I don't like it, she said.

Almost since the day we arrived I've noticed a change in Corrine. She isn't sick. She works as hard as ever. She is still sweet and good-natured. But sometimes I sense her spirit is being tested and that something in her is not at rest.

That's fine, I said. I'm glad you brought it up.

And don't let the children call you Mama Nettie, she said, even in play.

This bothered me a little, but I didn't say anything. The children do call me Mama Nettie sometimes because I do a good bit of fussing over them. But I never try to take Corrine's place.

And another thing, she said. I think we ought to try not to borrow each other's clothes.

Well, she never borrowed anything of mine because I don't have much. But I'm all the time borrowing something of hers.

You feeling yourself? I asked her.

She said yes.

I wish you could see my hut, Celie. I *love* it. Unlike our school, which is square, and unlike our church, which doesn't have walls – at least during the dry season – my hut is round, walled, with a round roofleaf roof. It is twenty steps across the middle and fits me to a T. Over the mud walls I have hung Olinka platters and mats and pieces of tribal cloth. The Olinka are known for their beautiful cotton fabric which they hand-weave and dye with berries, clay, indigo and tree bark. Then there is my paraffin camp stove in the center, and my camp bed to one side, covered with mosquito netting so that it almost looks like the bed of a bride. Then I have a small writing table where I write to you, a lamp, and a stool. Some wonderful rush mats on the floor. It is all colorful and warm and homey. My only desire for it now is a window! None of the village huts have windows, and when I spoke of a window to the women they laughed heartily. The rainy season makes the thought of a window ridiculous, apparently. But I am determined to have one, even if a flood collects daily on my floor.

I would give anything for a picture of you, Celie. In my trunk I have pictures donated to us by the missionary societies in England and America. Pictures of Christ, the Apostles, Mary, the Crucifixion. Speke, Livingstone. Stanley. Schweitzer. Maybe one day I'll put them up, but once, when I held them up to my fabric and mat covered walls they made me feel very small and unhappy, so I took them down. Even the picture of Christ which generally looks good anywhere looks peculiar here. We of course have all of these pictures hung in the school and many of Christ behind the altar at the church. That is enough, I think, though Samuel and Corrine have pictures and relics (crosses) in their hut as well.

Your sister,

Nettie

Dear Celie,

Tashi's mother and father were just here. They are upset because she spends so much time with Olivia. She is changing, becoming quiet and too thoughtful, they say. She is becoming someone else; her face is beginning to show the spirit of one of her aunts who was sold to the trader because she no longer fit into village life. This aunt refused to marry the man chosen for her. Refused to bow to the chief. Did nothing but lay up, crack cola nuts between her teeth and giggle.

They want to know what Olivia and Tashi do in my hut when all the other little girls are busy helping their mothers.

Is Tashi lazy at home? I asked.

The father looked at the mother. She said, No, on the contrary, Tashi works harder than most girls her age. And is quicker to finish her work. But it is only because she wishes to spend her afternoons with Olivia. She learns everything I teach her as if she already knows it, said the mother, but this knowledge does not really enter her soul.

The mother seemed puzzled and afraid.

The father, angry.

I thought: Aha. Tashi knows she is learning a way of life she will never live. But I did not say this.

The world is changing, I said. It is no longer a world just for boys and men.

Our women are respected here, said the father. We would never let them tramp the world as American women do. There is always someone to look after the Olinka woman. A father. An uncle. A brother or nephew. Do not be offended, Sister Nettie, but our people pity women such as you who are cast out, we know not from where, into a world unknown to you, where you must struggle all alone, for yourself.

So I am an object of pity and contempt, I thought, to men and women alike.

Furthermore, said Tashi's father, we are not simpletons. We understand that there are places in the world where women live differently from the way our women do, but we do not approve of this different way for our children.

But life is changing, even in Olinka, I said. We are here.

He spat on the ground. What are you? Three grownups and two children. In the rainy season some of you will probably die. You people do not last long in our climate. If you do not die, you will be weakened by illness. Oh, yes. We have seen it all before. You Christians come here, try hard to change us, get sick and go back to England, or wherever you come from. Only the trader on the coast remains, and even he is not the same white man, year in and year out. We know because we send him women.

Tashi is very intelligent, I said. She could be a teacher. A nurse. She could help the people in the village.

There is no place here for a woman to do those things, he said.

Then we should leave, I said. Sister Corrine and I.

No, no, he said.

Teach only the boys? I asked.

Yes, he said, as if my question was agreement.

There is a way that the men speak to women that reminds me too much of Pa. They listen just long enough to issue instructions. They don't even look at women when women are speaking. They look at the ground and bend their heads toward the ground. The women also do not 'look in a man's face' as they say. To 'look in a man's face' is a brazen thing to do. They look instead at his feet or his knees. And what can I say to this? Again, it is our own behavior around Pa.

Next time Tashi appears at your gate, you will send her straight home, her father said. Then he smiled. Your Olivia can visit her, and learn what women are for.

I smiled also. Olivia must learn to take her education about life where she can find it, I thought. His offer will make a splendid opportunity.

Goodbye until the next time, dear Celie, from a pitiful, cast-out woman who may perish during the rainy season.

Your loving sister,

Nettie

Dear Celie,

At first there was the faintest sound of movement in the forest. A kind of low humming. Then there was chopping and the sound of dragging. Then a scent, some days, of smoke. But now, after two months, during which I or the children or Corrine has been sick, all we hear is chopping and scraping and dragging. And every day we smell smoke.

Today one of the boys in my afternoon class burst out, as he entered, The road approaches! The road approaches! He had been hunting in the forest with his father and seen it.

Every day now the villagers gather at the edge of the village near the cassava fields, and watch the building of the road. And watching them, some on their stools and some squatted down on their haunches, all chewing cola nuts and making patterns in the dirt, I feel a great surge of love for them. For they do not approach the roadbuilders empty-handedly. Oh, no. Each day since they saw the road's approach they have been stuffing the roadbuilders with goat meat, millet mush, baked yam and cassava, cola nuts and palm wine. Each day is like a picnic, and I believe many friendships have been made, although the roadbuilders are from a different tribe some distance to the North and nearer the coast, and their language is somewhat different. I don't understand it, anyway, though the people of Olinka seem to. But they are clever people about most things, and understand new things very quickly.

It is hard to believe we've been here five years. Time

moves slowly, but passes quickly. Adam and Olivia are nearly as tall as me and doing very well in all their studies. Adam has a special aptitude for figures and it worries Samuel that soon he will have nothing more to teach him in this field, having exhausted his own knowledge.

When we were in England we met missionaries who sent their children back home when it was no longer possible to teach them in the bush. But it is hard to imagine life here without the children. They love the open feeling of the village, and love living in huts. They are excited by the hunting expertise of the men and the self-sufficiency of the women in raising their crops. No matter how down I may be, and sometimes I get very down indeed, a hug from Olivia or Adam completely restores me to the level of functioning, if nothing else. Their mother and I are not as close as we once were, but I feel more like their aunt than ever. And the three of us look more and more alike every day.

About a month ago, Corrine asked me not to invite Samuel to my hut unless she were present. She said it gave the villagers the wrong idea. This was a real blow to me because I treasure his company. Since Corrine almost never visits me herself I will have hardly anybody to talk to, just in friendship. But the children still come and sometimes spend the night when their parents want to be alone. I love those times. We roast groundnuts on my stove, sit on the floor and study maps of all the countries in the world. Sometimes Tashi comes over and tells stories that are popular among the Olinka children. I am encouraging her and Olivia to write them down in Olinka and English. It will be good practice for them. Olivia feels that, compared to Tashi, she has no good stories to tell. One day she started in on an 'Uncle Remus' tale only to discover Tashi had the original version of it! Her little face just fell. But then we got into a discussion of how Tashi's people's stories got to America, which fascinated Tashi. She cried when Olivia told how her grandmother had been treated as a slave.

No one else in this village wants to hear about slavery, however. They acknowledge no responsibility whatsoever. This is one thing about them that I definitely do not like.

We lost Tashi's father during the last rainy season. He fell ill with malaria and nothing the healer concocted saved him. He refused to take the medicine we use for it, or to let Samuel visit him at all. It was my first Olinka funeral. The women paint their faces white and wear white shroudlike garments and cry in a high keening voice. They wrapped the body in barkcloth and buried it under a big tree in the forest. Tashi was heartbroken. All her young life she has tried to please her father, never quite realizing that, as a girl, she never could. But the death brought her and her mother closer together, and now Catherine feels like one of us. By one of us I mean me and the children and sometimes Samuel. She is still in mourning and sticking close to her hut, but she says she will not marry again (since she already has five boy children she can now do whatever she wants. She has become an honorary man) and when I went to visit her she made it very clear that Tashi must continue to learn. She is the most industrious of all Tashi's father's widows, and her fields are praised for their cleanliness, productivity and general attractiveness. Perhaps I can help her with her work. It is in work that the women get to know and care about each other. It was through work that Catherine became friends with her husband's other wives.

This friendship among women is something Samuel often talks about. Because the women share a husband but the husband does not share their friendships, it makes Samuel uneasy. It *is* confusing, I suppose. And it *is* Samuel's duty as a Christian minister to preach the bible's directive of one husband and one wife. Samuel is confused because to him, since the women are friends and will do anything for one another – not always, but more often than anyone from America would expect – and since they giggle and gossip and nurse each other's children, then they must be happy with things as they are. But many of the women rarely spend time with their husbands. Some of them were promised to old or middle-aged men at birth. Their lives always center around work and their children and other women (since a woman cannot really have a man for a friend without the worst kind of ostracism and gossip). They indulge their husbands, if anything. You should just see how they make admiration over them. Praise their smallest accomplishments. Stuff them with palm wine and sweets. No wonder the men are often childish. And a grown child is a dangerous thing, especially since, among the Olinka, the husband has life and death power over the wife. If he accuses one of his wives of witchcraft or infidelity, she can be killed.

Thank God (and sometimes Samuel's intervention) this has not happened since we've been here. But the stories Tashi tells are often about such gruesome events that happened in the recent past. And God forbid that the child of a favorite wife should fall ill! That is the point at which even the women's friendships break down, as each woman fears the accusation of sorcery from the other, or from the husband.

Merry Christmas to you and yours, dear Celie. We celebrate it here on the 'dark' continent with prayer and song and a large picnic complete with watermelon, fresh fruit punch, and barbecue!

God bless you,
Nettie

Dearest Celie,

I meant to write you in time for Easter, but it was not a good time for me and I did not want to burden you with any distressing news. So a whole year has gone by. The first thing I should tell you about is the road. The road finally reached the cassava fields about nine months ago and the Olinka, who love nothing better than a celebration, outdid themselves preparing a feast for the roadbuilders who talked and laughed and cut their eyes at the Olinka women the whole day. In the evening many were invited into the village itself and there was merrymaking far into the night.

I think Africans are very much like white people back home, in that they think they are the center of the universe and that everything that is done is done for them. The Olinka definitely hold this view. And so they naturally thought the road being built was for them. And, in fact, the roadbuilders talked much of how quickly the Olinka will now be able to get to the coast. With a tarmac road it is only a three-day journey. By bicycle it will be even less. Of course no one in Olinka owns a bicycle, but one of the roadbuilders has one, and all the Olinka men covet it and talk of someday soon purchasing their own.

Well, the morning after the road was 'finished' as far as the Olinka were concerned (after all, it had reached their village), what should we discover but that the roadbuilders were back at work. They have instructions to continue the road for another thirty miles! And to continue it on its present course right through the village of Olinka. By the time we were out of bed, the road was already being dug through Catherine's newly planted yam field. Of course the Olinka were up in arms. But the roadbuilders were literally up in arms. They had guns, Celie, with orders to shoot!

It was pitiful, Celie. The people felt so betrayed! They stood by helplessly – they really don't know how to fight, and rarely think of it since the old days of tribal wars – as their crops and then their very homes were destroyed. Yes. The roadbuilders didn't deviate an inch from the plan the headman was following. Every hut that lay in the proposed roadpath was leveled. And, Celie, our church, our school, my hut, all went down in a matter of hours. Fortunately, we were able to save all of our things, but with a tarmac road running straight through the middle of it, the village itself seems gutted.

Immediately after understanding the roadbuilders' intentions, the chief set off toward the coast, seeking explanations and reparations. Two weeks later he returned with even more disturbing news. The whole territory, including the Olinkas' village, now belongs to a rubber manufacturer in England. As he neared the coast, he was stunned to see hundreds and hundreds of villagers much like the Olinka clearing the forests on each side of the road, and planting rubber trees. The ancient, giant mahogany trees, all the trees, the game, everything of the forest was being destroyed, and the land was forced to lie flat, he said, and bare as the palm of his hand.

At first he thought the people who told him about the English rubber company were mistaken, if only about its territory including the Olinka village. But eventually he was directed to the governor's mansion, a huge white building, with flags flying in its yard, and there had an audience with the white man in charge. It was this man who gave the roadbuilders their orders, this man who knew about the

Olinka only from a map. He spoke in English, which our chief tried to speak also.

It must have been a pathetic exchange. Our chief never learned English beyond an occasional odd phrase he picked up from Joseph, who pronounces 'English' 'Yanglush.'

But the worst was yet to be told. Since the Olinka no longer own their village, they must pay rent for it, and in order to use the water, which also no longer belongs to them, they must pay a water tax.

At first the people laughed. It really did seem crazy. They've been here forever. But the chief did not laugh.

We will fight the white man, they said.

But the white man is not alone, said the chief. He has brought his army.

That was several months ago, and so far nothing has happened. The people live like ostriches, never setting foot on the new road if they can help it, and never, ever, looking towards the coast. We have built another church and school. I have another hut. And so we wait.

Meanwhile, Corrine has been very ill with African fever. Many missionaries in the past have died from it.

But the children are fine. The boys now accept Olivia and Tashi in class and more mothers are sending their daughters to school. The men do not like it: who wants a wife who knows everything her husband knows? they fume. But the women have their ways, and they love their children, even their girls.

I will write more when things start looking up. I trust God they will.

Your sister,
Nettie

Dearest Celie,

This whole year, after Easter, has been difficult. Since Corrine's illness, all her work has fallen on me, and I must nurse her as well, which she resents.

One day when I was changing her as she lay in bed, she gave me a long, mean, but somehow pitiful look. Why do my children look like you? she asked.

Do you really think they look so much like me? I said.

You could have spit them out, she said.

Maybe just living together, loving people makes them look like you, I said. You know how much some old married people look alike.

Even these women saw the resemblance the first day we came, she said.

And that's worried you all this time? I tried to laugh it off.

But she just looked at me.

When did you first meet my husband? she wanted to know.

And that was when I knew what she thought. She thinks Adam and Olivia are my children, and that Samuel is their father!

Oh, Celie, this thing has been gnawing away at her all these years!

I met Samuel the same day I met you, Corrine, I said. (I still haven't got the hang of saying 'Sister' all the time.) As God is my witness, that's the truth.

Bring the bible, she said.

I brought the bible, and placed my hand on it, and swore.

You've never known me to lie, Corrine, I said. Please believe I am not lying now.

Then she called Samuel, and made him swear that the day she met me was the day he met me also.

He said: I apologize for this, Sister Nettie, please forgive us.

As soon as Samuel left the room she made me raise my dress and she sat up in her sickbed to examine my stomach.

I felt so sorry for her, and so humiliated, Celie. And the way she treats the children is the hardest part. She doesn't want them near her, which they don't understand. How could they? They don't even know they were adopted.

The village is due to be planted in rubber trees this coming season. The Olinka hunting territory has already been destroyed, and the men must go farther and farther away to find game. The women spend all their time in the fields, tending their crops and praying. They sing to the earth and to the sky and to their cassava and groundnuts. Songs of love and farewell.

We are all sad, here, Celie. I hope life is happier for you.

Your sister,

Nettie

Dear Celie,

Guess what? Samuel thought the children were mine too! That is why he urged me to come to Africa with them. When I showed up at their house he thought I was following my children, and, soft-hearted as he is, didn't have the heart to turn me away.

If they are not yours, he said, whose are they?

But I had some questions for him, first.

Where did you get them? I asked. And Celie, he told me a story that made my hair stand on end. I hope you, poor thing, are ready for it.

Once upon a time, there was a well-to-do farmer who owned his own property near town. Our town, Celie. And as he did so well farming and everything he turned his hand to prospered, he decided to open a store, and try his luck selling dry goods as well. Well, his store did so well that he talked two of his brothers into helping him run it, and, as the months went by, they were doing better and better. Then the white merchants began to get together and complain that this store was taking all the black business away from them, and the man's blacksmith shop that he set up behind the store, was taking some of the white. This would not do. And so, one night, the man's store was burned down, his smithy destroyed, and the man and his two brothers dragged out of their homes in the middle of the night and hanged.

The man had a wife whom he adored, and they had a little girl, barely two years old. She was also pregnant with another child. When the neighbors brought her husband's body home, it had been mutilated and burnt. The sight of it nearly killed her, and her second baby, also a girl, was born at this time. Although the widow's body recovered, her mind was never the same. She continued to fix her husband's plate at mealtimes just as she'd always done and was always full of talk about the plans she and her husband had made. The neighbors, though not always intending to, shunned her more and more, partly because the plans she talked about were grander than anything they could even conceive of for colored people, and partly because her attachment to the past was so pitiful. She was a good-looking woman, though, and still owned land, but there was no one to work it for her, and she didn't know how herself; besides she kept waiting for her husband to finish the meal she'd cooked for him and go to the fields himself. Soon there was nothing to eat that the neighbors did not bring, and she and her small children grubbed around in the yard as best they could.

While the second child was still a baby, a stranger appeared in the community, and lavished all his attention on the widow and her children; in a short while, they were married. Almost at once she was pregnant a third time, though her mental health was no better. Every year thereafter, she was pregnant, every year she became weaker and more mentally unstable, until, many years after she married the stranger, she died.

Two years before she died she had a baby girl that she was too sick to keep. Then a baby boy. These children were named Olivia and Adam.

This is Samuel's story, almost word for word.

The stranger who married the widow was someone Samuel had run with long before he found Christ. When the man showed up at Samuel's house with first Olivia and then Adam, Samuel felt not only unable to refuse the children, but as if God had answered his and Corrine's prayers.

He never told Corrine about the man or about the children's 'mother' because he hadn't wanted any sadness to cloud her happiness.

But then, out of nowhere, I appeared. He put two and two together, remembered that his old running buddy had always been a scamp, and took me in without any questions. Which, to tell the truth, had always puzzled me, but I put it down to Christian charity. Corrine had asked me once whether I was running away from home. But I explained I was a big girl now, my family back home very large and poor, and it was time for me to get out and earn my own living.

Tears had soaked my blouse when Samuel finished telling me all this. I couldn't begin, then, to tell him the truth. But Celie, I can tell you. And I pray with all my heart that you will get this letter, if none of the others.

Pa is not our pa!

Your devoted Sister,
Nettie

Dear God,

That's it, say Shug. Pack your stuff. You coming back to Tennessee with me.

But I feels daze.

My daddy lynch. My mama crazy. All my little half-brothers and sisters no kin to me. My children not my sister and brother. Pa not pa.

You must be sleep.

Dear Nettie,

For the first time in my life I wanted to see Pa. So me and Shug dress up in our new blue flower pants that match and big floppy Easter hats that match too, cept her roses red, mine yellow, and us clam in the Packard and glide over there. They put in paved roads all up and down the county now and twenty miles go like nothing.

I saw Pa once since I left home. One day me and Mr ——— was loading up the wagon at the feed store. Pa was with May Ellen and she was trying to fix her stocking. She was bent down over her leg and twisting the stocking into a knot above her knee, and he was standing over her tap-tap-tapping on the gravel with his cane. Look like he was thinking bout hitting her with it.

Mr ——— went up to them all friendly, with his hand stuck out, but I kept loading the wagon and looking at the patterns on the sacks. I never thought I'd ever want to see him again.

Well, it was a bright Spring day, sort of chill at first, like it be round Easter, and the first thing us notice soon as we turn into the lane is how green everything is, like even though the ground everywhere else not warmed up good, Pa's land is warm and ready to go. Then all along the road there's Easter lilies and jonquils and daffodils and all kinds of little early wildflowers. Then us notice all the birds singing they little cans off, all up and down the hedge, that itself is putting out little yellow flowers smell like Virginia creeper. It all so different from the rest of the country us drive through, it make us real quiet. I know this sound funny, Nettie, but even the sun seem to stand a little longer over our heads.

Well, say Shug, all this is pretty enough. You never said how pretty it was.

It wasn't this pretty, I say. Every Easter time it used to flood, and all us children had colds. Anyhow, I say, us stuck close to the house, and it sure ain't so hot.

That ain't so hot? she ast, as we swung up a long curving hill I didn't remember, right up to a big yellow two story house with green shutters and a steep green shingle roof.

I laughed. Us must have took the wrong turn, I say. This some white person's house.

It was so pretty though that us stop the car and just set looking at it.

What kind of trees all them flowering? ast Shug.

I don't know, I say. Look like peach, plum, apple, maybe cherry. But whatever they is, they sure pretty.

All round the house, all in back of it, nothing but blooming trees. Then more lilies and jonquils and roses clamming over everything. And all the time the little birds from all over the rest of the county sit up in these trees just going to town.

Finally, after us look at it awhile, I say, It so quiet, nobody home, I guess.

Naw, say Shug, probably in church. A nice bright Sunday like this.

Us better leave then, I say, before whoever it is lives here gits back. But just as I say that I notice my eye is staying on a fig tree it recognize, and us hear a car turning up the drive. Who should be in the car but Pa and some young girl look like his child.

He git out on his side, then go round to open the door for her. She dress to kill in a pink suit, big pink hat and pink shoes, a little pink purse hanging on her arm. They look at our license tag and then come up to the car. She put her hand through his arm.

Morning, he says, when he gits up to Shug's window.

Morning, she says slow, and I can tell he not what she expect.

Anything I can do for you? He ain't notice me and probably wouldn't even if he looked at me.

Shug say, under her breath, Is this him?

I say, Yeah.

What shock Shug and shock me too is how young he look. He look older than the child he with, even if she is dress up like a woman, but he look young for somebody to be anybody that got grown children and nearly grown grandchildren. But then I remember, he not my daddy, just my children daddy.

What your mama do, ast Shug, rob the cradle?

But he not so young.

I brought Celie, say Shug. Your daughter Celie. She wanted to visit you. Got some questions to ast.

He seem to think back a second. *Celie?* he say. Like, Who Celie? Then he say, Yall git out and come up on the porch. Daisy, he say to the little woman with him, go tell Hetty to hold dinner. She squeeze his arm, reach up and kiss him on the jaw. He turn his head and watch her go up the walk, up the steps, and through the front door. He follow us up the steps, up on the porch, help us pull out rocking chairs, then say, Now, what yall want?

The children here? I ast.

What children? he say. Then he laugh. Oh, they gone with they mama. She up and left me, you know. Went back to her folks. Yeah, he say, you would remember May Ellen.

Why she leave? I ast.

He laugh some more. Got too old for me, I reckon.

Then the little woman come back out and sit on the armrest of his chair. He talk to us and fondle her arm.

This Daisy, he say. My new wife.

Why, say Shug, you don't look more than fifteen.

I ain't, say Daisy.

I'm surprise your people let you marry.

She shrug, look at Pa. They work for him, she say. Live on his land.

I'm her people now, he say.

I feels so sick I almost gag. Nettie in Africa, I say. A missionary. She wrote me that you ain't our real Pa.

Well, he say. So now you know.

Daisy look at me with pity all over her face. It just like him to keep that from you, she say. He told me how he brought up two little girls that wasn't even his, she say. I don't think I really believed it, till now.

Naw, he never told them, say Shug.

What a old sweetie pie, say Daisy, kissing him on top the head. He fondle and fondle her arm. Look at me and grin.

Your daddy didn't know how to git along, he say. White-folks lynch him. Too sad a story to tell pitiful little growing girls, he say. Any man would have done what I done.

Maybe not, say Shug.

He look at her, then look at me. He can tell she know. But what do he care?

Take me, he say, I know how they is. The key to all of 'em is money. The trouble with our people is as soon as they got out of slavery they didn't want to give the white man nothing else. But the fact is, you got to give 'em something. Either your money, your land, your woman or your ass. So what I did was just right off offer to give 'em money. Before I planted a seed, I made sure this one and that one knowed one seed out of three was planted for *him*. Before I ground a grain of wheat, the same thing. And when I opened up your daddy's old store in town, I bought me my own white boy to run it. And what make it so good, he say, I bought him with whitefolks' money.

Ask the busy man your questions, Celie, say Shug. I think his dinner getting cold.

Where my daddy buried, I ast. That all I really want to know.

Next to your mammy, he say.

Any marker, I ast.

He look at me like I'm crazy. Lynched people don't git no marker, he say. Like this something everybody know.

Mama got one? I ast.

He say, Naw.

The birds sing just as sweet when us leave as when us come. Then, look like as soon as us turn back on the main road, they stop. By the time us got to the cemetery, the sky gray.

Us look and look for Ma and Pa. Hope for some scrap of wood that say something. But us don't find nothing but weeds and cockleburrs and paper flowers fading on some of the graves. Shug pick up a old horseshoe somebody horse lose. Us took that old horseshoe and us turned round and round together until we was dizzy enough to fall out, and where us would have fell us stuck the horseshoe in the ground.

Shug say, Us each other's peoples now, and kiss me.

Dear Celie,

I woke up this morning bound to tell Corrine and Samuel everything. I went over to their hut and pulled up a stool next to Corrine's bed. She's so weak by now that all she can do is look unfriendly — and I could tell I wasn't welcome.

I said, Corrine, I'm here to tell you and Samuel the truth.

She said, Samuel already told me. If the children yours, why didn't you just say so?

Samuel said, Now, honey.

She said, Don't Now Honey me. Nettie swore on the bible to tell me the truth. To tell God the truth, and she lied.

Corrine, I said, I didn't lie. I sort of turned my back more on Samuel and whispered: You saw my stomach, I said.

What do I know about pregnancy, she said. I never experienced it myself. For all I know, women may be able to rub out all the signs.

They can't rub out stretch marks, I said. Stretch marks go right into the skin, and a woman's stomach stretches enough so that it keeps a little pot, like all the women have here.

She turned her face to the wall.

Corrine, I said, I'm the children's aunt. Their mother is my older sister, Celie.

Then I told them the whole story. Only Corrine was still not convinced.

You and Samuel telling so many lies, who can believe anything you say? she asked.

You've got to believe Nettie, said Samuel. Though the part about you and Pa was a real shock to him.

Then I remembered what you told me about seeing Corrine and Samuel and Olivia in town, when she was buying cloth to make her and Olivia dresses, and how you sent me to her because she was the only woman you'd ever seen with money. I tried to make Corrine remember that day, but she couldn't.

She gets weaker and weaker, and unless she can believe us and start to feel something for her children, I fear we will lose her.

Oh, Celie, unbelief is a terrible thing. And so is the hurt we cause others unknowingly.

Pray for us,

Nettie

Dearest Celie,

Every day for the past week I've been trying to get Corrine to remember meeting you in town. I know if she can just recall your face, she will believe Olivia (if not Adam) is your child. They think Olivia looks like me, but that is only because I look like you. Olivia has your face and eyes, exactly. It amazes me that Corrine didn't see the resemblance.

Remember the main street of town? I asked. Remember the hitching post in front of Finley's dry goods store? Remember how the store smelled like peanut shells?

She says she remembers all this, but no men speaking to her.

Then I remember her quilts. The Olinka men make beautiful quilts which are full of animals and birds and people. And as soon as Corrine saw them, she began to make a quilt that alternated one square of appliqued figures with one nine-patch block, using the clothes the children had outgrown, and some of her old dresses.

I went to her trunk and started hauling out quilts.

Don't touch my things, said Corrine. I'm not gone yet.

I held up first one and then another to the light, trying to find the first one I remembered her making. And trying to remember, at the same time, the dresses she and Olivia were wearing the first months I lived with them.

Aha, I said, when I found what I was looking for, and laid the quilt across the bed.

Do you remember buying this cloth? I asked, pointing to a flowered square. And what about this checkered bird?

She traced the patterns with her finger, and slowly her eyes filled with tears.

She was so much like Olivia! she said. I was afraid she'd want her back. So I forgot her as soon as I could. All I let myself think about was how the clerk treated me! I was acting like somebody because I was Samuel's wife, and a Spelman Seminary graduate, and he treated me like any ordinary nigger. Oh, my feelings were hurt! And I was mad! And that's what I thought about, even told Samuel about, on the way home. Not about your sister – what was her name? – Celie? Nothing about her.

She began to cry in earnest. Me and Samuel holding her hands.

Don't cry. Don't cry, I said. My sister was glad to see Olivia with you. Glad to see her alive. She thought both her children were dead.

Poor thing! said Samuel. And we sat there talking a little and holding on to each other until Corrine fell off to sleep.

But, Celie, in the middle of the night she woke up, turned to Samuel and said: I believe. And died anyway.

Your Sister in Sorrow,

Nettie

Dearest Celie,

Just when I think I've learned to live with the heat, the constant dampness, even steaminess of my clothes, the swampiness under my arms and between my legs, my friend comes. And cramps and aches and pains – but I must still keep going as if nothing is happening, or be an embarrassment to Samuel, the children and myself. Not to mention the villagers, who think women who have their friends should not even be seen.

Right after her mother's death, Olivia got *her* friend; she and Tashi tend to each other is my guess. Nothing is said to me, in any event, and I don't know how to bring the subject up. Which feels wrong to me; but if you talk to an Olinka girl about her private parts, her mother and father will be annoyed, and it is very important to Olivia not to be looked upon as an outsider. Although the one ritual they do have to celebrate womanhood is so bloody and painful, I forbid Olivia to even think about it.

Do you remember how scared I was when it first happened to me? I thought I had cut myself. But thank God you were there to tell me I was all right.

We buried Corrine in the Olinka way, wrapped in barkcloth under a large tree. All of her sweet ways went with her. All of her education and a heart intent on doing good. She taught me so much! I know I will miss her always. The children were stunned by their mother's death. They knew she was very sick, but death is not something they think about in relation to their parents or themselves. It was a strange little procession. All of us in our white robes and with our faces painted white. Samuel is like someone lost. I don't believe they've spent a night apart since their marriage.

And how are you? dear Sister. The years have come and gone without a single word from you. Only the sky above us do we hold in common. I look at it often as if, somehow, reflected from its immensities, I will one day find myself gazing into your eyes. Your dear, large, clean and beautiful eyes. Oh, Celie! My life here is nothing but work, work, work, and worry. What girlhood I might have had passed me by. And I have nothing of my own. No man, no children, no close friend, except for Samuel. But I *do* have children, Adam and Olivia. And I *do* have friends, Tashi and Catherine. I even have a family – this village, which has fallen on such hard times.

Now the engineers have come to inspect the territory. Two white men came yesterday and spent a couple of hours strolling about the village, mainly looking at the wells. Such is the innate politeness of the Olinka that they rushed about preparing food for them, though precious little is left, since many of the gardens that flourish at this time of the year have been destroyed. And the white men sat eating as if the food was beneath notice.

It is understood by the Olinka that nothing good is likely to come from the same persons who destroyed their houses, but custom dies hard. I did not speak to the men myself, but Samuel did. He said their talk was all of workers, kilometers of land, rainfall, seedlings, machinery, and whatnot. One seemed totally indifferent to the people around him – simply eating and then smoking and staring off into the distance – and the other, somewhat younger, appeared to be enthusiastic about learning the language. Before, he says, it dies out.

I did not enjoy watching Samuel speaking to either of them. The one who hung on every word, or the one who looked through Samuel's head.

Samuel gave me all of Corrine's clothes, and I need them, though none of our clothing is suitable in this climate. This is true even of the clothing the Africans wear. They used to wear very little, but the ladies of England introduced the Mother Hubbard, a long, cumbersome, ill-fitting dress, completely shapeless, that inevitably gets dragged in the fire, causing burns aplenty. I have never been able to bring myself to wear one of these dresses, which all seem to have been made with giants in mind, so I was glad to have Corrine's things. At the same time, I dreaded putting them on. I remembered her saying we should stop wearing each other's clothes. And the memory pained me.

Are you sure Sister Corrine would want this? I asked Samuel.

Yes, Sister Nettie, he said. Try not to hold her fears against her. At the end she understood, and believed. And forgave — whatever there was to forgive.

I should have said something sooner, I said.

He asked me to tell him about you, and the words poured out like water. I was dying to tell someone about us. I told him about my letters to you every Christmas and Easter, and about how much it would have meant to us if he had gone to see you after I left. He was sorry he hesitated to become involved.

If only I'd understood then what I know now! he said.

But how could he? There is so much we don't understand. And so much unhappiness comes because of that.

love and Merry Christmas to you,
Your sister Nettie

Dear Nettie,

I don't write to God no more, I write to you.

What happen to God? ast Shug.

Who that? I say.

She look at me serious.

Big a devil as you is, I say, you not worried bout no God, surely.

She say, Wait a minute. Hold on just a minute here. Just because I don't harass it like some peoples us know don't mean I ain't got religion.

What God do for me? I ast.

She say, Celie! Like she shock. He gave you life, good health, and a good woman that love you to death.

Yeah, I say, and he give me a lynched daddy, a crazy mama, a lowdown dog of a step pa and a sister I probably won't ever see again. Anyhow, I say, the God I been praying and writing to is a man. And act just like all the other mens I know. Trifling, forgitful and lowdown.

She say, Miss Celie. You better hush. God might hear you.

Let 'im hear me, I say. If he ever listened to poor colored women the world would be a different place, I can tell you.

She talk and she talk, trying to budge me way from blasphemy. But I blaspheme much as I want to.

All my life I never care what people thought bout nothing I did, I say. But deep in my heart I care about God. What he going to think. And come to find out, he don't think. Just sit up there glorying in being deef, I reckon. But it ain't easy, trying to do without God. Even if you know he ain't there, trying to do without him is a strain.

I is a sinner, say Shug. Cause I was born. I don't deny it. But once you find out what's out there waiting for us, what else can you be?

Sinners have more good times, I say.

You know why? she ast.

Cause you ain't all the time worrying bout God, I say.

Naw, that ain't it, she say. Us worry bout God a lot. But once us feel loved by God, us do the best us can to please him with what us like.

You telling me God love you, and you ain't never done nothing for him? I mean, not go to church, sing in the choir, feed the preacher and all like that?

But if God love me, Celie, I don't have to do all that. Unless I want to. There's a lot of other things I can do that I speck God likes.

Like what? I ast.

Oh, she say. I can lay back and just admire stuff. Be happy. Have a good time.

Well, this sound like blasphemy sure nuff.

She say, Celie, tell the truth, have you ever found God in church? I never did. I just found a bunch of folks hoping for him to show. Any God I ever felt in church I brought in with me. And I think all the other folks did too. They come to church to *share* God, not find God.

Some folks didn't have him to share, I said. They the ones didn't speak to me while I was there struggling with my big belly and Mr —— children.

Right, she say.

Then she say: Tell me what your God look like, Celie.

Aw naw, I say. I'm too shame. Nobody ever ast me this before, so I'm sort of took by surprise. Besides, when I think about it, it don't seem quite right. But it all I got. I decide to stick up for him, just to see what Shug say.

Okay, I say. He big and old and tall and graybearded and white. He wear white robes and go barefooted.

Blue eyes? she ast.

Sort of bluish-grey. Cool. Big though. White lashes, I say.

She laugh.

Why you laugh? I ast. I don't think it so funny. What you expect him to look like, Mr ———?

That wouldn't be no improvement, she say. Then she tell me this old white man is the same God she used to see when she prayed. If you wait to find God in church, Celie, she say, that's who is bound to show up, cause that's where he live.

How come? I ast.

Cause that's the one that's in the white folks' white bible.

Shug! I say. God wrote the bible, white folks had nothing to do with it.

How come he look just like them, then? she say. Only bigger? And a heap more hair. How come the bible just like everything else they make, all about them doing one thing and another, and all the colored folks doing is gitting cursed?

I never thought bout that.

Nettie say somewhere in the bible it say Jesus' hair was like lamb's wool, I say.

Well, say Shug, if he came to any of these churches we talking bout he'd have to have it conked before anybody paid him any attention. The last thing niggers want to think about they God is that his hair kinky.

That's the truth, I say.

Ain't no way to read the bible and not think God white, she say. Then she sigh. When I found out I thought God was white, and a man, I lost interest. You mad cause he don't seem to listen to your prayers. Humph! Do the mayor listen to anything colored say? Ask Sofia, she say.

But I don't have to ast Sofia. I know white people never listen to colored, period. If they do, they only listen long enough to be able to tell you what to do.

Here's the thing, say Shug. The thing I believe. God is inside you and inside everybody else. You come into the world with God. But only them that search for it inside find it. And sometimes it just manifest itself even if you not looking, or don't know what you looking for. Trouble do it for most folks, I think. Sorrow, lord. Feeling like shit.

It? I ast.

Yeah, It. God ain't a he or a she, but a It.

But what do it look like? I ast.

Don't look like nothing, she say. It ain't a picture show. It ain't something you can look at apart from anything else, including yourself. I believe God is everything, say Shug. Everything that is or ever was or ever will be. And when you can feel that, and be happy to feel that, you've found it.

Shug a beautiful something, let me tell you. She frown a little, look out cross the yard, lean back in her chair, look like a big rose.

She say, My first step from the old white man was trees. Then air. Then birds. Then other people. But one day when I was sitting quiet and feeling like a motherless child, which I was, it come to me: that feeling of being part of everything, not separate at all. I knew that if I cut a tree, my arm would bleed. And I laughed and I cried and I run all round the house. I knew just what it was. In fact, when it happen, you can't miss it. It sort of like you know what, she say, grinning and rubbing high up on my thigh.

Shug! I say.

Oh, she say. God love all them feelings. That's some of the best stuff God did. And when you know God loves 'em you enjoys 'em a lot more. You can just relax, go with everything that's going, and praise God by liking what you like.

God don't think it dirty? I ast.

Naw, she say. God made it. Listen, God love everything you love – and a mess of stuff you don't. But more than anything else, God love admiration.

You saying God vain? I ast.

Naw, she say. Not vain, just wanting to share a good thing. I think it pisses God off if you walk by the color purple in a field somewhere and don't notice it.

What it do when it pissed off? I ast.

Oh, it make something else. People think pleasing God is all God care about. But any fool living in the world can see it always trying to please us back.

Yeah? I say.

Yeah, she say. It always making little surprises and springing them on us when us least expect.

You mean it want to be loved, just like the bible say.

Yes, Celie, she say. Everything want to be loved. Us sing and dance, make faces and give flower bouquets, trying to be loved. You ever notice that trees do everything to git attention we do, except walk?

Well, us talk and talk bout God, but I'm still adrift. Trying to chase that old white man out of my head. I been so busy thinking bout him I never truly notice nothing God make. Not a blade of corn (how it do that?) not the color purple (where it come from?). Not the little wildflowers. Nothing.

Now that my eyes opening, I feels like a fool. Next to any little scrub of a bush in my yard, Mr ———'s evil sort of shrink. But not altogether. Still, it is like Shug say, You have to git man off your eyeball, before you can see anything a'tall.

Man corrupt everything, say Shug. He on your box of grits, in your head, and all over the radio. He try to make you think he everywhere. Soon as you think he everywhere, you think he God. But he ain't. Whenever you trying to pray, and man plop himself on the other end of it, tell him to git lost, say Shug. Conjure up flowers, wind, water, a big rock.

But this hard work, let me tell you. He been there so long, he don't want to budge. He threaten lightening, floods and earthquakes. Us fight. I hardly pray at all. Every time I conjure up a rock, I throw it.

Amen

Dear Nettie,

When I told Shug I'm writing to you instead of to God, she laugh. Nettie don't know these people, she say. Considering who I been writing to, this strike me funny.

It was Sofia you saw working as the mayor's maid. The woman you saw carrying the white woman's packages that day in town. Sofia Mr ———'s son Harpo's wife. Polices lock her up for sassing the mayor's wife and hitting the mayor back. First she was in prison working in the laundry and dying fast. Then us got her move to the mayor's house. She had to sleep in a little room up under the house, but it was better than prison. Flies, maybe, but no rats.

Anyhow, they kept her eleven and a half years, give her six months off for good behavior so she could come home early to her family. Her bigger children married and gone, and her littlest children mad at her, don't know who she is. Think she act funny, look old and dote on that little white gal she raise.

Yesterday us all had dinner at Odessa's house. Odessa Sofia's sister. She raise the kids. Her and her husband Jack. Harpo's woman Squeak, and Harpo himself.

Sofia sit down at the big table like there's no room for her. Children reach cross her like she not there. Harpo and Squeak act like a old married couple. Children call Odessa mama. Call Squeak little mama. Call Sofia 'Miss.' The only one seem to pay her any tension at all is Harpo and Squeak's little girl, Suzie Q. She sit cross from Sofia and squinch up her eyes at her.

As soon as dinner over, Shug push back her chair and light a cigarette. Now is come the time to tell yall, she say.

Tell us what? Harpo ast.

Us leaving, she say.

Yeah? say Harpo, looking round for the coffee. And then looking over at Grady.

Us leaving, Shug say again. Mr —— look struck, like he always look when Shug say she going anywhere. He reach down and rub his stomach, look off side her head like nothing been said.

Grady say, Such good peoples, that's the truth. The salt of the earth. But – time to move on.

Squeak not saying nothing. She got her chin glued to her plate. I'm not saying nothing either. I'm waiting for the feathers to fly.

Celie is coming with us, say Shug.

Mr ——'s head swivel back straight. Say what? he ast.

Celie is coming to Memphis with me.

Over my dead body, Mr —— say.

You satisfied that what you want, Shug say, cool as clabber.

Mr —— start up from his seat, look at Shug, plop back down again. He look over at me. I thought you was finally happy, he say. What wrong now?

You a lowdown dog is what's wrong, I say. It's time to leave you and enter into the Creation. And your dead body just the welcome mat I need.

Say what? he ast. Shock.

All round the table folkses mouths be dropping open.

You took my sister Nettie away from me, I say. And she was the only person love me in the world.

Mr —— start to sputter. ButButButButBut. Sound like some kind of motor.

But Nettie and my children coming home soon, I say. And when she do, all us together gon whup your ass.

Nettie and your children! say Mr ———. You talking crazy.

I got children, I say. Being brought up in Africa. Good schools, lots of fresh air and exercise. Turning out a heap better than the fools you didn't even try to raise.

Hold on, say Harpo.

Oh, hold on hell, I say. If you hadn't tried to rule over Sofia the white folks never would have caught her.

Sofia so surprise to hear me speak up she ain't chewed for ten minutes.

That's a lie, say Harpo.

A little truth in it, say Sofia.

Everybody look at her like they surprise she there. It like a voice speaking from the grave.

You was all rotten children, I say. You made my life a hell on earth. And your daddy here ain't dead horse's shit.

Mr ——— reach over to slap me. I jab my case knife in his hand.

You bitch, he say. What will people say, you running off to Memphis like you don't have a house to look after?

Shug say, Albert. Try to think like you got some sense. Why any woman give a shit what people think is a mystery to me.

Well, say Grady, trying to bring light. A woman can't git a man if peoples talk.

Shug look at me and us giggle. Then us laugh sure nuff. Then Squeak start to laugh. Then Sofia. All us laugh and laugh.

Shug say, Ain't they something? Us say um *hum*, and slap the table, wipe the water from our eyes.

Harpo look at Squeak. Shut up Squeak, he say. It bad luck for women to laugh at men.

She say, Okay. She sit up straight, suck in her breath, try to press her face together.

He look at Sofia. She look at him and laugh in his face. I

already had my bad luck, she say. I had enough to keep me laughing the rest of my life.

Harpo look at her like he did the night she knock Mary Agnes down. A little spark fly cross the table.

I got six children by this crazy woman, he mutter.

Five, she say.

He so outdone he can't even say, Say what?

He look over at the youngest child. She sullen, mean, mischeevous and too stubborn to live in this world. But he love her best of all. Her name Henrietta.

Henrietta, he say.

She say, Yesssss. . . like they say it on the radio.

Everything she say confuse him. Nothing, he say. Then he say, Go git me a cool glass of water.

She don't move.

Please, he say.

She go git the water, put it by his plate, give him a peck on the cheek. Say, Poor Daddy. Sit back down.

You not gitting a penny of my money, Mr —— say to me. Not one thin dime.

Did I ever ast you for money? I say. I never ast you for nothing. Not even for your sorry hand in marriage.

Shug break in right there. Wait, she say. Hold it. Somebody else going with us too. No use in Celie being the only one taking the weight.

Everybody sort of cut they eyes at Sofia. She the one they can't quite find a place for. She the stranger.

It ain't me, she say, and her look say, Fuck you for entertaining the thought. She reach for a biscuit and sort of root her behind deeper into her seat. One look at this big stout graying, wildeyed woman and you know not even to ast. Nothing.

But just to clear this up neat and quick, she say, I'm home. Period.

Her sister Odessa come and put her arms round her. Jack move up close.

Course you is, Jack say.

Mama crying? ast one of Sofia children.

Miss Sofia too, another one say.

But Sofia cry quick, like she do most things.

Who going? she ast.

Nobody say nothing. It so quiet you can hear the embers dying back in the stove. Sound like they falling in on each other.

Finally, Squeak look at everybody from under her bangs. Me, she say. I'm going North.

You going What? say Harpo. He so surprise. He begin to sputter, sputter, just like his daddy. Sound like I don't know what.

I want to sing, say Squeak.

Sing! say Harpo.

Yeah, say Squeak. Sing. I ain't sung in public since Jolentha was born. Her name Jolentha. They call her Suzie Q.

You ain't had to sing in public since Jolentha was born. Everything you need I done provided for.

I need to sing, say Squeak.

Listen Squeak, say Harpo. You can't go to Memphis. That's all there is to it.

Mary Agnes, say Squeak.

Squeak, Mary Agnes, what difference do it make?

It make a lot, say Squeak. When I was Mary Agnes I could sing in public.

Just then a little knock come on the door.

Odessa and Jack look at each other. Come in, say Jack.

A skinny little white woman stick most of herself through the door.

Oh, you all are eating dinner, she say. Excuse me.

That's all right, say Odessa. Us just finishing up. But

there's plenty left. Why don't you sit down and join us. Or I could fix you something to eat on the porch.

Oh lord, say Shug.

It Eleanor Jane, the white girl Sofia used to work for.

She look round till she spot Sofia, then she seem to let her breath out. No thank you, Odessa, she say. I ain't hungry. I just come to see Sofia.

Sofia, she say. Can I see you on the porch for a minute.

All right, Miss Eleanor, she say. Sofia push back from the table and they go out on the porch. A few minutes later us hear Miss Eleanor sniffling. Then she really boo-hoo.

What the matter with her? Mr —— ast.

Henrietta say, Prob-limbszzzz . . . like somebody on the radio.

Odessa shrug. She always underfoot, she say.

A lot of drinking in that family, say Jack. Plus, they can't keep that boy of theirs in college. He get drunk, aggravate his sister, chase women, hunt niggers, and that ain't all.

That enough, say Shug. Poor Sofia.

Pretty soon Sofia come back in and sit down.

What the matter? ast Odessa.

A lot of mess back at the house, say Sofia.

You got to go back up there? Odessa ast.

Yeah, say Sofia. In a few minutes. But I'll try to be back before the children go to bed.

Henrietta ast to be excuse, say she got a stomach ache.

Squeak and Harpo's little girl come over, look up at Sofia, say, You gotta go Misofia?

Sofia say, Yeah, pull her up on her lap. Sofia on parole, she say. Got to act nice.

Suzie Q lay her head on Sofia chest. Poor Sofia, she say, just like she heard Shug. Poor Sofia.

Mary Agnes, darling, say Harpo, look how Suzie Q take to Sofia.

Yeah, say Squeak, children know good when they see it. She and Sofia smile at one nother.

Go on sing, say Sofia, I'll look after this one till you come back.

You will? say Squeak.

Yeah, say Sofia.

And look after Harpo, too, say Squeak. Please ma'am.

Amen

Dear Nettie,

Well, you know wherever there's a man, there's trouble. And it seem like, going to Memphis, Grady was all over the car. No matter which way us change up, he want to sit next to Squeak.

While me and Shug sleeping and he driving, he tell Squeak all about life in North Memphis, Tennessee. I can't half sleep for him raving bout clubs and clothes and forty-nine brands of beer. Talking so much bout stuff to drink make me have to pee. Then us have to find a road going off into the bushes to relieve ourselves.

Mr —— try to act like he don't care I'm going.

You'll be back, he say. Nothing up North for nobody like you. Shug got talent, he say. She can sing. She got spunk, he say. She can talk to anybody. Shug got looks, he say. She can stand up and be notice. But what you got? You ugly. You skinny. You shape funny. You too scared to open your mouth to people. All you fit to do in Memphis is be Shug's maid. Take out her slop-jar and maybe cook her food. You not that good a cook either. And this house ain't been clean good since my first wife died. And nobody crazy or backward enough to want to marry you, neither. What you gon do? Hire yourself out to farm? He laugh. Maybe somebody let you work on they railroad.

Any more letters come? I ast.

He say, What?

You heard me, I say. Any more letters from Nettie come?

If they did, he say, I wouldn't give 'em to you. You two of a kind, he say. A man try to be nice to you, you fly in his face.

I curse you, I say.

What that mean? he say.

I say, Until you do right by me, everything you touch will crumble.

He laugh. Who you think you is? he say. You can't curse nobody. Look at you. You black, you pore, you ugly, you a woman. Goddam, he say, you nothing at all.

Until you do right by me, I say, everything you even dream about will fail. I give it to him straight, just like it come to me. And it seem to come to me from the trees.

Whoever heard of such a thing, say Mr ———. I probably didn't whup your ass enough.

Every lick you hit me you will suffer twice, I say. Then I say, You better stop talking because all I'm telling you ain't coming just from me. Look like when I open my mouth the air rush in and shape words.

Shit, he say. I should have lock you up. Just let you out to work.

The jail you plan for me is the one in which you will rot, I say.

Shug come over to where us talking. She take one look at my face and say Celie! Then she turn to Mr ———. Stop Albert, she say. Don't say no more. You just going to make it harder on yourself.

I'll fix her wagon! say Mr ———, and spring toward me.

A dust devil flew up on the porch between us, fill my mouth with dirt. The dirt say, Anything you do to me, already done to you.

Then I feel Shug shake me. Celie, she say. And I come to myself.

I'm pore, I'm black, I may be ugly and can't cook, a voice say to everything listening. But I'm here.

Amen, say Shug. Amen, amen.

Dear Nettie,

So what is it like in Memphis? Shug's house is big and pink and look sort of like a barn. Cept where you would put hay, she got bedrooms and toilets and a big ballroom where she and her band sometime work. She got plenty grounds round the house and a bunch of monuments and a fountain out front. She got statues of folks I never heard of and never hope to see. She got a whole bunch of elephants and turtles everywhere. Some big, some little, some in the fountain, some up under the trees. Turtles and elephants. And all over her house. Curtains got elephants, bedspreads got turtles.

Shug give me a big back bedroom overlook the backyard and the bushes down by the creek.

I know you use to morning sun, she say.

Her room right cross from mine, in the shade. She work late, sleep late, git up late. No turtles or elephants on her bedroom furniture, but a few statues spread out round the room. She sleep in silks and satins, even her sheets. And her bed round!

I wanted to build me a round house, say Shug, but everybody act like that's backward. You can't put windows in a round house, they say. But I made me up some plans, anyway. One of these days ... she say, showing me the papers.

It a big round pink house, look sort of like some kind of fruit. It got windows and doors and a lot of trees round it.

What it made of? I ast.

Mud, she say. But I wouldn't mind concrete. I figure you could make the molds for each section, pour the concrete in, let it get hard, knock off the mold, glue the parts together somehow and you'd have your house.

Well, I like this one you got, I say. That one look a little small.

It ain't bad, say Shug. But I just feel funny living in a square. If I was square, then I could take it better, she say.

Us talk bout houses a lot. How they built, what kind of wood people use. Talk about how to make the outside around your house something you can use. I sit down on the bed and start to draw a kind of wood skirt around her concrete house. You can sit on this, I say, when you get tired of being in the house.

Yeah, she say, and let's put awning over it. She took the pencil and put the wood skirt in the shade.

Flower boxes go here, she say, drawing some.

And geraniums in them, I say, drawing some.

And a few stone elephants right here, she say.

And a turtle or two right here.

And how us know you live here too? she ast.

Ducks! I say.

By the time us finish our house look like it can swim or fly.

Nobody cook like Shug when she cook.

She get up early in the morning and go to market. Buy only stuff that's fresh. Then she come home and sit on the back step humming and shelling peas or cleaning collards or fish or whatever she bought. Then she git all her pots going at once and turn on the radio. By one o'clock everything ready and she call us to the table. Ham and greens and chicken and cornbread. Chitlins and blackeyed peas and souse. Pickled okra and watermelon rind. Caramel cake and blackberry pie.

Us eat and eat, and drink a little sweet wine and beer too.

Then Shug and me go fall out in her room to listen to music till all that food have a chance to settle. It cool and dark in her room. Her bed soft and nice. Us lay with our arms round each other. Sometimes Shug read the paper out loud. The news always sound crazy. People fussing and fighting and pointing fingers at other people, and never even looking for no peace.

People insane, say Shug. Crazy as betsy bugs. Nothing built this crazy can last. Listen, she say. Here they building a dam so they can flood out a Indian tribe that been there since time. And look at this, they making a picture bout that man that kilt all them women. The same man that play the killer is playing the priest. And look at these shoes they making now, she say. Try to walk a mile in a pair of them, she say. You be limping all the way home. And you see what they trying to do with that man that beat the Chinese couple to death. Nothing whatsoever.

Yeah, I say, but some things pleasant.

Right, say Shug, turning the page. Mr and Mrs Hamilton Hufflemeyer are pleased to announce the wedding of their daughter June Sue. The Morrises of Endover Road are spearheading a social for the Episcopal church. Mrs Herbert Edenfail was on a visit last week to the Adirondacks to see her ailing mother, the former Mrs Geoffrey Hood.

All these faces look happy enough, say Shug. Big and beefy. Eyes clear and innocent, like they don't know them other crooks on the front page. But they the same folks, she say.

But pretty soon, after cooking a big dinner and making a to-do about cleaning the house, Shug go back to work. That mean she never give a thought to what she eat. Never give a thought to where she sleep. She on the road somewhere for weeks at a time, come home with bleary eyes, rotten breath, overweight and sort of greasy. No place hardly to stop and really wash herself, especially her hair, on the road.

Let me go with you, I say. I can press your clothes, do your hair. It would be like old times, when you was singing at Harpo's.

She say, Naw. She can act like she not bored in front of a audience of strangers, a lot of them white, but she wouldn't have the nerve to try to act in front of me.

Besides, she say. You not my maid. I didn't bring you to Memphis to be that. I brought you here to love you and help you get on your feet.

And now she off on the road for two weeks, and me and Grady and Squeak rattle round the house trying to get our stuff together. Squeak been going round to a lot of clubs and Grady been taking her. Plus he seem to be doing a little farming out back the house.

I sit in the dining room making pants after pants. I got pants now in every color and size under the sun. Since us started making pants down home, I ain't been able to stop. I change the cloth, I change the print, I change the waist, I change the pocket. I change the hem, I change the fullness of the leg. I make so many pants Shug tease me. I didn't know what I was starting, she say, laughing. Pants all over her chairs, hanging all in front of the china closet. Newspaper patterns and cloth all over the table and the floor. She come home, kiss me, step over all the mess. Say, before she leave again, How much money you think you need *this* week?

Then finally one day I made the perfect pair of pants. For my sugar, naturally. They soft dark blue jersey with teeny patches of red. But what make them so good is, they totally comfortable. Cause Shug eat a lot of junk on the road, and drink, her stomach bloat. So the pants can be let out without messing up the shape. Because she have to pack her stuff and fight wrinkles, these pants are soft, hardly wrinkle at all, and the little figures in the cloth always look perky and bright. And they full round the ankle so if she want to sing in 'em and wear 'em sort of like a long dress, she can. Plus, once Shug put them on, she knock your eyes out.

Miss Celie, she say. You is a wonder to behold.

I duck my head. She run round the house looking at herself in mirrors. No matter how she look, she look good.

You know how it is when you don't have nothing to do, I say, when she brag to Grady and Squeak bout her pants. I sit here thinking bout how to make a living and before I know it I'm off on another pair pants.

By now Squeak see a pair *she* like. Oh, Miss Celie, she say. Can I try on those?

She put on a pair the color of sunset. Orangish with a little greyish fleck. She come back out looking just fine. Grady look at her like he could eat her up.

Shug finger the pieces of cloth I got hanging on everything. It all soft, flowing, rich and catch the light. This a far cry from that stiff army shit us started with, she say. You ought to make up a special pair to thank and show Jack.

What she say that for. The next week I'm in and out of stores spending more of Shug's money. I sit looking out cross the yard trying to see in my mind what a pair of pants for Jack would look like. Jack is tall and kind and don't hardly say anything. Love children. Respect his wife, Odessa, and all Odessa amazon sisters. Anything she want to take on, he right there. Never talking much, though. That's the main thing. And then I remember one time he touch me. And it felt like his fingers had eyes. Felt like he knew me all over, but he just touch my arm up near the shoulder.

I start to make pants for Jack. They have to be camel. And soft and strong. And they have to have big pockets so he can keep a lot of children's things. Marbles and string and pennies and rocks. And they have to be washable and they have to fit closer round the leg than Shug's so he can run if he need to snatch a child out the way of something. And they have to be something he can lay back in when he hold Odessa in front of the fire. And . . .

I dream and dream and dream over Jack's pants. And cut and sew. And finish them. And send them off.

Next thing I hear, Odessa want a pair.

Then Shug want two more pair just like the first. Then everybody in her band want some. Then orders start to come in from everywhere Shug sing. Pretty soon I'm swamp.

One day when Shug come home, I say, You know, I love doing this, but I got to git out and make a living pretty soon. Look like this just holding me back.

She laugh. Let's us put a few advertisements in the paper, she say. And let's us raise your prices a hefty notch. And let's us just go ahead and give you this diningroom for your factory and git you some more women in here to cut and sew, while you sit back and design. You making your living, Celie, she say. Girl, you on your way.

Nettie, I am making some pants for you to beat the heat in Africa. Soft, white, thin. Drawstring waist. You won't ever have to feel too hot and overdress again. I plan to make them by hand. Every stitch I sew will be a kiss.

> Amen,
> Your Sister, Celie
> Folkspants, Unlimited.
> Sugar Avery Drive
> Memphis, Tennessee

Dear Nettie,

I am so happy. I got love, I got work, I got money, friends and time. And you alive and be home soon. With our children.

Jerene and Darlene come help me with the business. They twins. Never married. Love to sew. Plus, Darlene trying to teach me how to talk. She say US not so hot. A dead country give-away. You say US where most folks say WE, she say, and peoples think you dumb. Colored peoples think you a hick and white folks be amuse.

What I care? I ast. I'm happy.

But she say I feel more happier talking like she talk. Can't nothing make me happier than seeing you again, I think, but I don't say nothing. Every time I say something the way I say it, she correct me until I say it some other way. Pretty soon it feel like I can't think. My mind run up on a thought, git confuse, run back and sort of lay down.

You sure this worth it? I ast.

She say Yeah. Bring me a bunch of books. Whitefolks all over them, talking bout apples and dogs.

What I care bout dogs? I think.

Darlene keep trying. Think how much better Shug feel with you educated, she say. She won't be shame to take you anywhere.

Shug not shame no how, I say. But she don't believe this the truth. Sugar, she say one day when Shug home, don't you think it be nice if Celie could talk proper?

Shug say, She can talk in sign language for all I care. She make herself a nice cup of herb tea and start talking bout hot oiling her hair.

But I let Darlene worry on. Sometimes I think bout the apples and the dogs, sometimes I don't. Look like to me only a fool would want you to talk in a way that feel peculiar to your mind. But she sweet and she sew good and us need something to haggle over while us work.

I'm busy making pants for Sofia now. One leg be purple, one leg be red. I dream Sofia wearing these pants, one day she was jumping over the moon.

Amen,
Your sister, Celie

Dear Nettie,

Walking down to Harpo and Sofia house it feel just like old times. Cept the house new, down below the juke-joint, and it a lot bigger than it was before. Then too I feels different. Look different. Got on some dark blue pants and a white silk shirt that look righteous. Little red flat-heel slippers, and a flower in my hair. I pass Mr —— house and him sitting up on the porch and he didn't even know who I was.

Just when I raise my hand to knock, I hear a crash. Sound like a chair falling over. Then I hear arguing.

Harpo say, Whoever heard of women pallbearers. That all I'm trying to say.

Well, say Sofia, you said it. Now you can hush.

I know she your mother, say Harpo. But still.

You gon help us or not? say Sofia.

What it gon look like? say Harpo. Three big stout women pallbearers look like they ought to be home frying chicken.

Three of our brothers be with us, on the other side, say Sofia. I guess they look like field hands.

But peoples use to men doing this sort of thing. Women weaker, he say. People think they weaker, say they weaker, anyhow. Women spose to take it easy. Cry if you want to. Not try to take over.

Try to take over, say Sofia. The woman dead. I can cry and take it easy and lift the coffin too. And whether you help us or not with the food and the chairs and the get-together afterward, that's exactly what I plan to do.

It git real quiet. After while Harpo say, real soft to Sofia, Why you like this, huh? Why you always think you have to do things your own way? I ast your mama bout it one time, while you was in jail.

What she say? ast Sofia.

She say you think your way as good as anybody else's. Plus, it yours.

Sofia laugh.

I know my timing bad, but I knock anyhow.

Oh, Miss Celie, say Sofia, flinging open the screen. How good you look. Don't she look good, Harpo? Harpo stare at me like he never seen me before.

Sofia give me a big hug and kiss me on the jaw. Where Miss Shug? she ast.

She on the road, I say. But she was real sorry to hear your mama pass.

Well, say Sofia, Mama fight the good fight. If there's a glory anywhere she right in the middle of it.

How you, Harpo? I ast. Still eating?

He and Sofia laugh.

I don't reckon Mary Agnes could come back this time, say Sofia. She was just here bout a month ago. You just ought to see her and Suzie Q.

Naw, I say. She finally working steady, singing at two or three clubs round town. Folks love her a lot.

Suzie Q so proud of her, she say. Love her singing. Love her perfume. Love her dresses. Love to wear her hats and shoes.

How she doing in school? I ast.

Oh, she fine, say Sofia. Smart as a little whip. Once she got over being mad her mama left her and found out I was Henrietta's real mama, she was all right. She dote on Henrietta.

How Henrietta?

Evil, say Sofia. Little face always look like stormy weather. But maybe she'll grow out of it. It took her daddy forty years to learn to be pleasant. He used to be nasty to his own ma.

Yall see much of him? I ast.

Bout as much as us see of Mary Agnes, say Sofia.

Mary Agnes not the same, say Harpo.

What you mean? I ast.

I don't know, he say. Her mind wander. She talk like she drunk. And every time she turn round look like she want to see Grady.

They both smoke a lot of reefer, I say.

Reefer, say Harpo. What kind of a thing is that?

Something make you feel good, I say. Something make you see visions. Something make your love come down. But if you smoke it too much it make you feebleminded. Confuse. Always need to clutch hold of somebody. Grady grow it in the backyard, I say.

I never heard of such a thing, say Sofia. It grow in the ground?

Like a weed, I say. Grady got half a acre if he got a row.

How big it git? ast Harpo.

Big, I say. Way up over my head. And bushy.

And what part they smoke?

The leaf, I say.

And they smoke up all that? he ast.

I laugh. Naw, he sell most of it.

You ever taste it? he ast.

Yeah, I say. He make it up in cigarettes, sell 'em for a dime. It rot your breath, I say, but yall want to try one?

Not if it make us crazy, say Sofia. It hard enough to git by without being a fool.

It just like whiskey, I say. You got to stay ahead of it. You know a little drink now and then never hurt nobody, but when you can't git started without asking the bottle, you in trouble.

You smoke it much, Miss Celie? Harpo ast.

Do I look like a fool? I ast. I smoke when I want to talk to God. I smoke when I want to make love. Lately I feel like me and God make love just fine anyhow. Whether I smoke reefer or not.

Miss Celie! say Sofia. Shock.

Girl, I'm bless, I say to Sofia. God know what I mean.

Us sit round the kitchen table and light up. I show 'em how to suck in they wind. Harpo git strangle. Sofia choke.

Pretty soon Sofia say, That funny, I never heard that humming before.

What humming? Harpo ast.

Listen, she say.

Us git real quiet and listen. Sure enough, us hear ummmmmmmm.

What it coming from? ast Sofia. She git up and go look out the door. Nothing there. Sound git louder Ummmmmmm.

Harpo go look out the window. Nothing out there, he say. Humming say UMMMMMMM.

I think I know what it is, I say.

They say, What?

I say, Everything.

Yeah, they say. That make a lots of sense.

Well, say Harpo at the funeral, here come the amazons.

Her brothers there too, I whisper back. What you call them?

I don't know, he say. Them three always stood by they crazy sisters. Nothing yet could get 'em to budge. I wonder what they wives have to put up with.

They all march stoutly in, shaking the church, and place Sofia mother in front the pulpit.

Folks crying and fanning and trying to keep a stray eye on they children, but they don't stare at Sofia and her sisters. They act like this the way it always done. I love folks.

Amen

Dear Nettie,

The first thing I notice bout Mr —— is how clean he is. His skin shine. His hair brush back.

When he walk by the casket to review Sofia mother's body he stop, whisper something to her. Pat her shoulder. On his way back to his seat he look over at me. I raise my fan and look off the other way.

Us went back to Harpo's after the funeral.

I know you won't believe this, Miss Celie, say Sofia, but Mr —— act like he trying to git religion.

Big a devil as he is, I say, trying is bout all he can do.

He don't go to church or nothing, but he not so quick to judge. He work real hard too.

What? I say. Mr —— work!

He sure do. He out there in the field from sunup to sundown. And clean that house just like a woman.

Even cook, say Harpo. And what more, wash the dishes when he finish.

Naw, I say. Yall must still be dope.

But he don't talk much or be round people, Sofia say.

Sound like craziness closing in to me, I say.

Just then, Mr —— walk up.

How you Celie, he say.

Fine, I say. I look in his eyes and I see he feeling scared of me. Well, good, I think. Let him feel what I felt.

Shug didn't come with you this time? he say.

Naw, I say. She have to work. Sorry bout Sofia mama though.

Anybody be sorry, he say. The woman that brought Sofia in the world brought something.

I don't say nothing.

They put her away nice, he say.

They sure did, I say.

And so many grandchildren, he say. Well. Twelve children, all busy multiplying. Just the family enough to fill the church.

Yeah, I say. That's the truth.

How long you here for? he say.

Maybe a week, I say.

You know Harpo and Sofia baby girl real sick? he say.

Naw, I didn't, I say. I point to Henrietta in the crowd. There she is over there, I say. She look just fine.

Yeah, she look fine, he say, but she got some kind of blood disease. Blood sort of clot up in her veins every once in a while, make her sick as a dog. I don't think she gon make it, he say.

Great goodness of life, I say.

Yeah, he say. It hard for Sofia. She still have to try to prop up that white gal she raise. Now her mama dead. Her health not that good either. Plus, Henrietta a hard row to hoe whether she sick or well.

Oh, she a little mess, I say. Then I think back to one of Nettie's letters bout the sicknesses children have where she at in Africa. Seem like to me she mention something bout blood clots. I try to remember what she say African peoples do, but I can't. Talking to Mr ―― such a surprise I can't think of nothing. Not even nothing else to say.

Mr ―― stand waiting for me to say something, looking off up to his house. Finally he say, Good evening, and walk away.

Sofia say after I left, Mr ―― live like a pig. Shut up in

the house so much it stunk. Wouldn't let nobody in until finally Harpo force his way in. Clean the house, got food. Give his daddy a bath. Mr —— too weak to fight back. Plus, too far gone to care.

He couldn't sleep, she say. At night he thought he heard bats outside the door. Other things rattling in the chimney. But the worse part was having to listen to his own heart. It did pretty well as long as there was daylight, but soon as night come, it went crazy. Beating so loud it shook the room. Sound like drums.

Harpo went up there plenty nights to sleep with him, say Sofia. Mr —— would be all cram up in a corner of the bed. Eyes clamp on different pieces of furniture, see if they move in his direction. You know how little he is, say Sofia. And how big and stout Harpo is. Well, one night I walked up to tell Harpo something – and the two of them was just laying there on the bed fast asleep. Harpo holding his daddy in his arms.

After that, I start to feel again for Harpo, Sofia say. And pretty soon us start work on our new house. She laugh. But did I say it been easy? If I did, God would make me cut my own switch.

What make him pull through? I ast.

Oh, she say, Harpo made him send you the rest of your sister's letters. Right after that he start to improve. You know meanness kill, she say.

Amen

Dearest Celie,

By now I expected to be home. Looking into your face and saying Celie, is it really you? I try to picture what the years have brought you in the way of weight and wrinkles – or how you fix your hair. From a skinny, hard little something I've become quite plump. And some of my hair is gray!

But Samuel tells me he loves me plump and graying.

Does this surprise you?

We were married last Fall in England where we tried to get relief for the Olinka from the churches and the Missionary Society.

As long as they could, the Olinka ignored the road and the white builders who came. But eventually they had to notice them because one of the first things the builders did was tell the people they must be moved elsewhere. The builders wanted the village site as headquarters for the rubber plantation. It is the only spot for miles that has a steady supply of fresh water.

Protesting and driven, the Olinka, along with their missionaries, were placed on a barren stretch of land that has no water at all for six months of the year. During that time, they must buy water from the planters. During the rainy season there is a river and they are trying to dig holes in the nearby rocks to make cisterns. So far they collect water in discarded oil drums, which the builders brought.

But the most horrible thing to happen had to do with the roofleaf, which, as I must have written you, the people worship as a God and which they use to cover their huts. Well, on this barren strip of ground the planters erected workers' barracks. One for men and one for women and children. But, because the Olinka swore they would never live in a dwelling not covered by their God, Roofleaf, the builders left these barracks uncovered. Then they proceeded to plow under the Olinka village and everything else for miles around. Including every last stalk of roofleaf.

After nearly unbearable weeks in the hot sun, we were awakened one morning by the sound of a large truck pulling into the compound. It was loaded with sheets of corrugated tin.

Celie, we had to *pay* for the tin. Which exhausted what meager savings the Olinka had, and nearly wiped out the money Samuel and I had managed to put by for the education of the children once we return home. Which we have planned to do each year since Corrine died, only to find ourselves more and more involved in the Olinka's problems. Nothing could be uglier than corrugated tin, Celie. And as they struggled to put up roofs of this cold, hard, glittery, ugly metal the women raised a deafening ululation of sorrow that echoed off the cavern walls for miles around. It was on this day that the Olinka acknowledged at least temporary defeat.

Though the Olinka no longer ask anything of us, beyond teaching their children – because they can see how powerless we and our God are – Samuel and I decided we must do something about this latest outrage, even as many of the people to whom we felt close ran away to join the *mbeles* or forest people, who live deep in the jungle, refusing to work for whites or be ruled by them.

So off we went, with the children, to England.

It was an incredible voyage, Celie, not only because we had almost forgot about the rest of the world, and such things as ships and coal fires and streetlights and oatmeal, but because on the ship with us was the white woman missionary whom we'd heard about years ago. She was now retired from missionary work and going back to England to live. She was traveling with a little African boy whom she introduced as her grandchild!

Of course it is impossible to ignore the presence of an aging white woman accompanied by a small black child. The ship was in a tither. Each day she and the child walked about the deck alone, groups of white people falling into silence as they passed.

She is a jaunty, stringy, blue-eyed woman, with hair the color of silver and dry grass. A short chin, and when she speaks she seems to be gargling.

I'm pushing on for sixty-five, she told us, when we found ourselves sharing a table for dinner one night. Been in the tropics most of my life. But, she said, a big war is coming. Bigger than the one they were starting when I left. It'll go hard on England, but I expect we'll survive. I missed the other war, she said. I mean to be present for this one.

Samuel and I had never really thought about war.

Why, she said, the signs are all over Africa. India too, I expect. First there's a road built to where you keep your goods. Then your trees are hauled off to make ships and captain's furniture. Then your land is planted with something you can't eat. Then you're forced to work it. That's happening all over Africa, she said. Burma too, I expect.

But Harold here and I decided to get out. Didn't we Harry? she said, giving the little boy a biscuit. The child said nothing, just chewed his biscuit thoughtfully. Adam and Olivia soon took him off to explore the lifeboats.

Doris' story – the woman's name is Doris Baines – is an interesting one. But I won't bore you with it as we eventually became bored.

She was born to great wealth in England. Her father was

Lord Somebody or Other. They were forever giving or attending parties that were no fun. Besides, she wanted to write books. Her family were against it. Totally. They hoped she'd marry.

Me *marry*! she hooted. (Really, she has the oddest ideas.)

They did everything to convince me, she said. You can't imagine. I never saw so many milkfed young men in all my life as when I was nineteen and twenty. Each one more boring than the last. Can anything *be* more boring than an upper-class Englishman? she said. They remind one of bloody mushrooms.

Well, she rattled on, through endless dinners, because the captain assigned us permanently to the same table. It seems the notion of becoming a missionary struck her one evening she was getting ready for yet another tedious date, and lay in the tub thinking a convent would be better than the castle in which she lived. She could think, she could write. She could be her own boss. But wait. As a nun she would not be her own boss. God would be boss. The virgin mother. The mother superior. Etc. Etc. Ah, but a missionary! Far off in the wilds of India, alone! It seemed like bliss.

And so she cultivated a pious interest in heathens. Fooled her parents. Fooled the Missionary Society, who were so taken with her quick command of languages they sent her to Africa (worst luck!) where she began writing novels about everything under the sun.

My pen name is Jared Hunt, she said. In England and even in America, I'm a run-away success. Rich, famous. An eccentric recluse who spends most of his time shooting wild game.

Well now, she continued, several evenings later, you don't think I paid much attention to the heathen? I saw nothing wrong with them as they were. And they seemed to like *me* well enough. I was actually able to help them a good deal. I was a writer, after all, and I wrote reams of paper on their behalf: about their culture, their behavior, their needs, that sort of thing. You'd be surprised how good writing matters when you're going after money. I learned to speak their language faultlessly, and to throw off the missionary snoopers back at headquarters I wrote entire reports in it. I tapped the family vaults for close on to a million pounds before I got anything from the missionary societies or rich old family friends. I built a hospital, a grammar school. A college. A swimming pool – the one luxury I permitted myself, since swimming in the river one is subject to attack by leeches.

You wouldn't believe the peace! she said, at breakfast, halfway to England. Within a year everything as far as me and the heathen were concerned ran like clockwork. I told them right off that their souls were no concern of mine, that I wanted to write books and not be disturbed. For this pleasure I was prepared to pay. Rather handsomely.

In a burst of appreciation one day, I'm afraid the chief – not knowing what else to do, no doubt – presented me with a couple of wives. I don't think it was commonly believed I was a woman. There seemed some question in their minds just what I was. Anyhow. I educated the two young girls as best I could. Sent them to England, of course, to learn medicine and agriculture. Welcomed them home when they returned, gave them away in marriage to two young chaps who were always about the place, and began the happiest period of my life as the grandmother of their children. I must say, she beamed, I've turned out to be fab-o as a grand*mama*. I learned it from the Akweans. They never spank their children. Never lock them away in another part of the hut. They do a bit of bloody cutting around puberty. But Harry's mother the doctor is going to change all that. Isn't she Harold?

Anyway, she said. When I get to England I'll put a stop to

their bloody encroachments. I'll tell them what to do with their bloody road and their bloody rubber plantations and their bloody sunburned but still bloody boring English planters and engineers. I am a very wealthy woman, and I *own* the village of Akwee.

We listened to most of this in more or less respectful silence. The children were very taken with young Harold, though he never said a word in our presence. He seemed fond of his grandmother and used to her, but her verbosity produced in him a kind of soberly observant speechlessness.

He's quite different with us though, said Adam, who is really a great lover of children, and could get through to any child given half an hour. Adam makes jokes, he sings, he clowns and knows games. And he has the sunniest smile, most of the time – and great healthy African teeth.

As I write about his sunny smile I realize he's been unusually glum during this trip. Interested and excited, but not really *sunny*, except when he's with young Harold.

I will have to ask Olivia what's wrong. She is thrilled at the thought of going back to England. Her mother used to tell her about the thatched cottages of the English and how they reminded her of the roofleaf huts of the Olinka. They are square, though, she'd say. More like our church and school than like our homes, which Olivia thought very strange.

When we reached England, Samuel and I presented the Olinka's grievances to the bishop of the English branch of our church, a youngish man wearing spectacles who sat thumbing through a stack of Samuel's yearly reports. Instead of even mentioning the Olinka the bishop wanted to know how long it had been since Corrine's death, and why, as soon as she died, I had not returned to America.

I really did not understand what he was driving at.

Appearances, Miss ——, he said. Appearances. What must the natives think?

About what? I asked.

Come, come, he said.

We behave as brother and sister to each other, said Samuel.

The bishop smirked. Yes, he did.

I felt my face go hot.

Well, there was more of this, but why burden you with it? You know what some people are, and the bishop was one of them. Samuel and I left without even a word about the Olinka's problems.

Samuel was so angry, I was frightened. He said the only thing for us to do, if we wanted to remain in Africa, was join the *mbeles* and encourage all the Olinka to do the same.

But suppose they do not want to go? I asked. Many of them are too old to move back into the forest. Many are sick. The women have small babies. And then there are the youngsters who want bicycles and British clothes. Mirrors and shiny cooking pots. They want to work for the white people in order to have these things.

Things! he said, in disgust. Bloody *things*!

Well, we have a month here anyway, I said, let's make the most of it.

Because we had spent so much of our money on tin roofs and the voyage over, it had to be a poor man's month in England. But it was a very good time for us. We began to feel ourselves a family, without Corrine. And people meeting us on the street never failed (if they spoke to us at all) to express the sentiment that the children looked just like the two of us. The children began to accept this as natural, and began going out to view the sights that interested them, alone. Leaving their father and me to our quieter, more sedate pleasures, one of which was simple conversation.

Samuel, of course, was born in the North, in New York, and grew up and was educated there. He met Corrine through his aunt who had been a missionary, along with Corrine's aunt, in the Belgian Congo. Samuel frequently accompanied his aunt Althea to Atlanta, where Corrine's aunt Theodosia lived.

These two ladies had been through marvelous things together, said Samuel, laughing. They'd been attacked by lions, stampeded by elephants, flooded out by rains, made war on by 'natives.' The tales they told were simply incredible. There they sat on a heavily antimacassared horsehair sofa, two prim and proper ladies in ruffles and lace, telling these stupendous stories over tea.

Corrine and I as teenagers used to attempt to stylize these tales into comics. We called them such things as THREE MONTHS IN A HAMMOCK, or SORE HIPS OF THE DARK CONTINENT. Or, A MAP OF AFRICA: A GUIDE TO NATIVE INDIFFERENCE TO THE HOLY WORD.

We made fun of them, but we were riveted on their adventures, and on the ladies' telling of them. They were so staid looking. So proper. You really couldn't imagine them actually building – with their own hands – a school in the bush. Or battling reptiles. Or unfriendly Africans who thought, since they were wearing dresses with things that looked like wings behind, they should be able to fly.

Bush? Corrine would snicker to me or me to her. And just the sound of the word would send us off into quiet hysteria, while we calmly sipped our tea. Because of course they didn't realize they were being funny, and to us they were, very. And of course the prevailing popular view of Africans at that time contributed to our feeling of amusement. Not only were Africans savages, they were bumbling, inept savages, rather like their bumbling, inept brethren at home. But we carefully, not to say studiously, avoided this very apparent connection.

Corrine's mother was a dedicated housewife and mother who disliked her more adventurous sister. But she never prevented Corrine from visiting. And when Corrine was old enough, she sent her to Spelman Seminary where Aunt Theodosia had gone. This was a very interesting place. It was started by two white missionaries from New England who used to wear identical dresses. Started in a church basement, it soon moved up to Army barracks. Eventually these two ladies were able to get large sums of money from some of the richest men in America, and so the place grew. Buildings, trees. Girls were taught everything: Reading, Writing, Arithmetic, sewing, cleaning, cooking. But more than anything else, they were taught to serve God and the colored community. Their official motto was OUR WHOLE SCHOOL FOR CHRIST. But I always thought their unofficial motto should have been OUR COMMUNITY COVERS THE WORLD, because no sooner had a young woman got through Spelman Seminary than she began to put her hand to whatever work she could do for her people, anywhere in the world. It was truly astonishing. These very polite and proper young women, some of them never having set foot outside their own small country towns, except to come to the Seminary, thought nothing of packing up for India, Africa, the Orient. Or for Philadelphia or New York.

Sixty years or so before the founding of the school, the Cherokee Indians who lived in Georgia were forced to leave their homes and walk, through the snow, to resettlement camps in Oklahoma. A third of them died on the way. But many of them refused to leave Georgia. They hid out as colored people and eventually blended with us. Many of these mixed-race people were at Spelman. Some remembered who they actually were, but most did not. If they thought about it at all (and it became harder to think about Indians because there were none around) they thought they were yellow or reddish brown and wavy haired because of white ancestors, not Indian.

Even Corrine thought this, he said. And yet, I always felt her Indianness. She was so quiet. So reflective. And she could erase herself, her spirit, with a swiftness that truly startled, when she knew the people around her could not respect it.

It did not seem hard for Samuel to talk about Corrine while we were in England. It wasn't hard for me to listen.

It all seems so improbable, he said. Here I am, an aging man whose dreams of helping people have been just that, dreams. How Corrine and I as children would have laughed at ourselves. TWENTY YEARS A FOOL OF THE WEST, or MOUTH AND ROOFLEAF DISEASE: A TREATISE ON FUTILITY IN THE TROPICS. Etc. Etc. We failed so utterly, he said. We became as comical as Althea and Theodosia. I think her awareness of this fueled Corrine's sickness. She was far more intuitive than I. Her gift for understanding people much greater. She used to say the Olinka resented us, but I wouldn't see it. But they do, you know.

No, I said, it isn't resentment, exactly. It really is indifference. Sometimes I feel our position is like that of flies on an elephant's hide.

I remember once, before Corrine and I were married, Samuel continued, Aunt Theodosia had one of her at-homes. She had them every Thursday. She'd invited a lot of 'serious young people' as she called them, and one of them was a young Harvard scholar named Edward. DuBoyce was his last name, I think. Anyhow, Aunt Theodosia was going on about her African adventures, leading up to the time King Leopold of Belgium presented her with a medal. Well Edward, or perhaps his name was Bill, was a very impatient sort. You saw it in his eyes, you could see it in the way he moved his body. He was never still. As Aunt Theodosia got closer to the part about her surprise and joy over receiving this medal – which validated her service as an exemplary missionary in the King's colony – DuBoyce's foot began to pat the floor rapidly and uncontrollably. Corrine and I looked at each other in alarm. Clearly this man had heard this tale before and was not prepared to endure it a second time.

Madame, he said, when Aunt Theodosia finished her story and flashed her famous medal around the room, do you realize King Leopold cut the hands off workers who, in the opinion of his plantation overseers, did not fulfill their rubber quota? Rather than cherish that medal, Madame, you should regard it as a symbol of your unwitting complicity with this despot who worked to death and brutalized and eventually exterminated thousands and thousands of African peoples.

Well, said Samuel, silence struck the gathering like a blight. Poor Aunt Theodosia! There's something in all of us that wants a medal for what we have done. That wants to be appreciated. And Africans certainly don't deal in medals. They hardly seem to care whether missionaries exist.

Don't be bitter, I said.

How can I not? he said.

The Africans never asked us to come, you know. There's no use blaming them if we feel unwelcome.

It's worse than unwelcome, said Samuel. The Africans don't even see us. They don't even recognize us as the brothers and sisters they sold.

Oh, Samuel, I said. Don't.

But you know, he had started to cry. Oh Nettie, he said. That's the heart of it, don't you see. We love them. We try every way we can to show that love. But they reject us. They never even listen to how we've suffered. And if they listen they say stupid things. Why don't you speak our language? they ask. Why can't you remember the old ways? Why aren't you happy in America, if everyone there drives motorcars?

Celie, it seemed as good a time as any to put my arms around him. Which I did. And words long buried in my heart crept to my lips. I stroked his dear head and face and I called him darling and dear. And I'm afraid, dear, dear Celie, that concern and passion soon ran away with us.

I hope when you receive this news of your sister's forward behavior you will not be shocked or inclined to judge me harshly. Especially when I tell you what a total joy it was. I was transported by ecstasy in Samuel's arms.

You may have guessed that I loved him all along; but I did not know it. Oh, I loved him as a brother and respected him as a friend, but Celie, I love him bodily, *as a man*! I love his walk, his size, his shape, his smell, the kinkiness of his hair. I love the very texture of his palms. The pink of his inner lip. I love his big nose. I love his brows. I love his feet. And I love his dear eyes in which the vulnerability and beauty of his soul can be plainly read.

The children saw the change in us immediately. I'm afraid, my dear, we were radiant.

We love each other dearly, Samuel told them, with his arm around me. We intend to marry.

But before we do, I said, I must tell you something about my life and about Corrine and about someone else. And it was then I told them about you, Celie. And about their mother Corrine's love of them. And about being their aunt.

But where is this other woman, your sister? asked Olivia.

I explained your marriage to Mr —— as best I could.

Adam was instantly alarmed. He is a very sensitive soul who hears what isn't said as clearly as what is.

We will go back to America soon, said Samuel to reassure him, and see about her.

The children stood up with us in a simple church ceremony in London. And it was that night, after the wedding dinner, when we were all getting ready for bed, that Olivia told me what has been troubling her brother. He is missing Tashi.

But he's also very angry with her, she said, because when we left, she was planning to scar her face.

I didn't know this. One of the things we thought we'd helped stop was the scarring or cutting of tribal marks on the faces of young women.

It is a way the Olinka can show they still have their own ways, said Olivia, even though the white man has taken everything else. Tashi didn't want to do it, but to make her people feel better, she's resigned. She's going to have the female initiation ceremony too, she said.

Oh, no, I said. That's so dangerous. Suppose she becomes infected?

I know, said Olivia. I told her nobody in America or Europe cuts off pieces of themselves. And anyway, she should have had it when she was eleven, if she was going to have it. She's too old for it now.

Well, some men are circumcized, I said, but that's just the removal of a bit of skin.

Tashi was happy that the initiation ceremony isn't done in Europe or America, said Olivia. That makes it even more valuable to her.

I see, I said.

She and Adam had an awful fight. Not like any they've had before. He wasn't teasing her or chasing her around the village or trying to tie roofleaf twigs in her hair. He was mad enough to strike her.

Well, it's a good thing he didn't, I said. Tashi would have jammed his head through her rug loom.

I'll be glad when we get back home, said Olivia. Adam isn't the only one who misses Tashi.

She kissed me and her father good night. Adam soon came in to do the same.

Mama Nettie, he said, sitting on the bed next to me, how do you know when you really love someone?

Sometimes you don't know, I said.

He is a beautiful young man, Celie. Tall and broad-shouldered, with a deep, thoughtful voice. Did I tell you he writes verses? And loves to sing? He's a son to make you proud.

Your loving sister,
Nettie

P.S. Your brother Samuel sends his love as well.

Dearest Celie,

When we returned home everyone seemed happy to see us. When we told them our appeal to the church and the Missionary Society failed, they were disappointed. They literally wiped the smiles off their faces along with the sweat, and returned, dejected, to their barracks. We went on to our building, a combination church, house and school, and began to unpack our things.

The children . . . I realize I shouldn't call them children, they're grown, went in search of Tashi; an hour later they returned dumbfounded. They discovered no sign of her. Catherine, her mother, is planting rubber trees some distance from the compound, they were told. But no one had seen Tashi all day.

Olivia was very disappointed. Adam was trying to appear unconcerned, but I noticed he was absentmindedly biting the skin around his nails.

After two days it became clear that Tashi was deliberately hiding. Her friends said while we were away she'd undergone both the facial scarification ceremony and the rite of female initiation. Adam went quite gray at this news. Olivia merely stricken and more concerned than ever to find her.

It was not until Sunday that we saw Tashi. She'd lost a considerable amount of weight, and seemed listless, dull-eyed and tired. Her face was still swollen from half a dozen small, neat incisions high on each cheek. When she put out her hand to Adam he refused to take it. He just looked at her scars, turned on his heel and left.

She and Olivia hugged. But it was a quiet, heavy embrace. Nothing like the boisterous, giggling behavior I expect from them.

Tashi is, unfortunately, ashamed of these scars on her face, and now hardly ever raises her head. They must be painful too because they look irritated and red.

But this is what the villagers are doing to the young women and even the men, Carving their identification as a people into their children's faces. But the children think of scarification as backward, something from their grandparents' generation, and often resist. So the carving is done by force, under the most appalling conditions. We provide antiseptics and cotton and a place for the children to cry and nurse their wounds.

Each day Adam presses us to leave for home. He can no longer bear living as we do. There aren't even any trees near us, just giant boulders and smaller rocks. And more and more of his companions are running away. The real reason, of course, is he can no longer bear his conflicting feelings about Tashi, who is beginning, I think, to appreciate the magnitude of her mistake.

Samuel and I are truly happy, Celie. And so grateful to God that we are! We still keep a school for the littlest children; those eight and over are already workers in the fields. In order to pay rent for the barracks, taxes on the land, and to buy water and wood and food, everyone must work. So, we teach the young ones, babysit the babies, look after the old and sick, and attend birthing mothers. Our days are fuller than ever, our sojourn in England already a dream. But all things look brighter because I have a loving soul to share them with.

Your sister,
Nettie

Dearest Nettie,

The man us knowed as Pa is dead.

How come you still call him Pa? Shug ast me the other day.

But, too late to call him Alphonso. I never even remember Ma calling him by his name. She always said, Your Pa. I reckon to make us believe it better. Anyhow, his little wife, Daisy, call me up on the telephone in the middle of the night.

Miss Celie, she say, I got bad news. Alphonso dead.

Who? I ast.

Alphonso, she say. Your stepdaddy.

How he die? I ast. I think of killing, being hit by a truck, struck by lightening, lingering disease. But she say, Naw, he died in his sleep. Well, not quite in his sleep, she say. Us was spending a little time in bed together, you know, before us drop off.

Well, I say, you have my sympathy.

Yes ma'am, she say, and I thought I had this house too, but look like it belong to your sister Nettie and you.

Say what? I ast.

Your stepdaddy been dead over a week, she say. When us went to town to hear the will read yesterday, you could have knock me over with a feather. Your real daddy owned the land and the house and the store. He left it to your mama. When your mama died, it passed on to you and your sister Nettie. I don't know why Alphonso never told you that.

Well, I say, anything coming from him, I don't want it.

I hear Daisy suck in her breath. How about your sister Nettie, she say. You think she feel the same way?

I wake up a little bit then. By the time Shug roll over and ast me who it is, I'm beginning to see the light.

Don't be a fool, Shug say, nudging me with her foot. You got your own house now. Your daddy and mama left it for you. That dog of a stepdaddy just a bad odor passing through.

But I never had no house, I say. Just to think about having my own house enough to scare me. Plus, this house I'm gitting is bigger than Shug's, got more land around it. And, it come with a store.

My God, I say to Shug. Me and Nettie own a drygood store. What us gon sell?

How bout pants? she say.

So us hung up the phone and rush down home again to look at the property.

About a mile before us got to town us come up on the entrance to the colored cemetery. Shug was sound asleep, but something told me I ought to drive in. Pretty soon I see something look like a short skyscraper and I stop the car and go up to it. Sure enough it's got Alphonso's name on it. Got a lot of other stuff on it too. Member of this and that. Leading businessman and farmer. Upright husband and father. Kind to the poor and helpless. He been dead two weeks but fresh flowers still blooming on his grave.

Shug git out the car and come stand by me.

Finally she yawn loud and stretch herself. The son of a bitch still dead, she say.

Daisy try to act like she glad to see us, but she not. She got two children and look pregnant with one more. But she got nice clothes, a car, and Alphonso left her all his money. Plus, I think she manage to set her folks up while she live with him.

She say, Celie, the old house you remember was torn down

so Alphonso could build this one. He got an Atlanta architect to design it, and these tiles come all the way from New York. We was standing in the kitchen at the time. But he put tiles everywhere. Kitchen, toilet, back porch. All around the fireplaces in back and front parlour. But this, the house, go with the place, right on, she say. Of course I did take the furniture, because Alphonso bought it special for me.

Fine with me, I say. I can't get over having a house. Soon as Daisy leave me with the keys I run from one room to another like I'm crazy. Look at this, I say to Shug. Look at that! She look, she grin. She hug me whenever she git the chance and I stand still.

You doin' all right, Miss Celie, she say. God know where you live.

Then she took some cedar sticks out of her bag and lit them and gave one of them to me. Us started at the very top of the house in the attic, and us smoked it all the way down to the basement, chasing out all the evil and making a place for good.

Oh, Nettie, us have a house! A house big enough for us and our children, for your husband and Shug. Now you can come home cause you have a home to come to!

Your loving sister,
Celie

Dear Nettie,

My heart broke.

Shug love somebody else.

Maybe if I had stayed in Memphis last summer it never would have happen. But I spent the summer fixing up the house. I thought if you come anytime soon, I want it to be ready. And it is real pretty, now, and comfortable. And I found me a nice lady to live in it and look after it. Then I come home to Shug.

Miss Celie, she say, how would you like some Chinese food to celebrate your coming home?

I loves Chinese food. So off us go to the restaurant. I'm so excited bout being home again I don't even notice how nervous Shug is. She a big graceful woman most of the time, even when she mad. But I notice she can't git her chopsticks to work right. She knock over her glass of water. Somehow or nother her eggroll come unravel.

But I think she just so glad to see me. So I preen and pose for her and stuff myself with wonton soup and fried rice.

Finally the fortune cookies come. I love fortune cookies. They so cute. And I read my fortune right away. It say, because you are who you are, the future look happy and bright.

I laugh. Pass it on to Shug. She look at it and smile. I feel at peace with the world.

Shug pull her slip of paper out real slow, like she scared of what might be on it.

Well? I say, watching her read it. What it say?

She look down at it, look up at me. Say, It say I got the hots for a boy of nineteen.

Let me see, I say, laughing. And I read it out loud. A burnt finger remember the fire, it say.

I'm trying to tell you, Shug say.

Trying to tell me what? I'm so dense it still don't penetrate. For one thing, it been a long time since I thought about boys and I ain't never thought about men.

Last year, say Shug, I hired a new man to work in the band. I almost didn't because he can't play nothing but flute. And who ever heard of blues flute? I hadn't. The very notion sound crazy. But it was just my luck that blues flute is the one thing blues music been lacking and the minute I heard Germaine play I knew this for a fact.

Germaine? I ast.

Yeah, she say, Germaine. I don't know who give him that flittish name, but it suit him.

Then she start right in to rave about this boy. Like all his good points have to be stuff I'm dying to hear.

Oh, she say. He little. He cute. Got nice buns. You know, real Bantu. She so used to telling me everything she rattle on and on, gitting more excited and in-love looking by the minute. By the time she finish talking bout his neat little dancing feet and git back up to his honey brown curly hair, I feel like shit.

Hold it, I say. Stop. Shug, you killing me.

She halt in mid-praise. Her eyes fill with tears and her face crumple. Oh God, Celie, she say. I'm sorry. I just been dying to tell somebody, and you the somebody I usually tell.

Well, I say, if words could kill, I'd be in the ambulance.

She put her face in her hands and start to cry. Celie, she say, through her fingers, I still love you.

But I just sit there and watch her. Seem like all my wonton soup turn to ice.

Why you so upset? she ast, when us got back home. You never seem to git upset bout Grady. And he was my husband.

Grady never bring no sparkle to your eye, I think. But I don't say nothing. I'm too far away.

Course, she say, Grady so dull, Jesus. And when you finish talking bout women and reefer you finish Grady. But still, she say.

I don't say nothing.

She try to laugh. I was so glad he lit out after Mary Agnes I didn't know what to do, she say. I don't know who tried to teach him what to do in the bedroom, but it must have been a furniture salesman.

I don't say nothing. Stillness, coolness. Nothingness. Coming fast.

You notice when they left here together going to Panama I didn't shed a tear? But now really, she say, what they gon look like in Panama?

Poor Mary Agnes, I think. How could anybody guess old dull Grady would end up running a reefer plantation in Panama?

Course they making boocoos of money, say Shug. And Mary Agnes outdress everybody down there, the way she tell it in her letters. And at least Grady let her sing. What little snatches of her songs she can still remember. But really, she say, Panama? Where is it at, anyhow? Is it down there round Cuba? Us ought to go to Cuba, Miss Celie, you know? Lots of gambling there and good times. A lots of colored folks look like Mary Agnes. Some real black, like us. All in the same family though. Try to pass for white, somebody mention your grandma.

I don't say nothing. I pray to die, just so I don't never have to speak.

All right, say Shug. It started when you was down home.

I missed you, Celie. And you know I'm a high natured woman.

I went and got a piece of paper that I was using for cutting patterns. I wrote her a note. It said, Shut up.

But Celie, she say. I have to make you understand. Look, she say. I'm gitting old. I'm fat. Nobody think I'm good looking no more, but you. Or so I thought. He's nineteen. A baby. How long can it last?

He's a man. I write on the paper.

Yeah, she say. He is. And I know how you feel about men. But I don't feel that way. I would never be fool enough to take any of them seriously, she say, but some mens can be a lots of fun.

Spare me, I write.

Celie, she say. All I ast is six months. Just six months to have my last fling. I got to have it Celie. I'm too weak a woman not to. But if you just give me six months, Celie, I will try to make our life together like it was.

Not hardly. I write.

Celie, she say, Do you love me? She down on her knees by now, tears falling all over the place. My heart hurt so much I can't believe it. How can it keep beating, feeling like this? But I'm a woman. I love you, I say. Whatever happen, whatever you do, I love you.

She whimper a little, lean her head against my chair. Thank you, she say.

But I can't stay here, I say.

But Celie, she say, how can you leave me? You're my friend. I love this child and I'm scared to death. He's a third of my age. A third of my size. Even a third of my color. She try to laugh again. You know he gon hurt me worse than I'm hurting you. Don't leave me, please.

Just then the door bell ring. Shug wiped her face and went to answer it, saw who it was and kept on out the door. Soon

I heard a car drive off. I went on up to bed. But sleep remain a stranger to this night.

Pray for me,
Your sister, Celie

Dear Nettie,

The only thing keep me alive is watching Henrietta fight for her life. And boy can she fight. Every time she have an attack she scream enough to wake the dead. Us do what you say the peoples do in Africa. Us feed her yams every single day. Just our luck she hate yams and she not too polite to let us know. Everybody for miles around try to come up with yam dishes that don't taste like yams. Us git plates of yam eggs, yam chitlins, yam goat. And soup. My God, folks be making soup out of everything but shoe leather trying to kill off the yam taste. But Henrietta claim she still taste it, and is likely to throw whatever it is out the window. Us tell her in a little while she'll have three months not to eat yams, but she say that day don't seem like it ever want to come. Meanwhile, her joints all swole, she hot enough to burn, she say her head feel like its full of little white men with hammers.

Sometime I meet up with Mr —— visiting Henrietta. He dream up his own little sneaky recipes. For instance, one time he hid the yams in peanut butter. Us sit by the fire with Harpo and Sofia and play a hand or two of bid whist, while Suzie Q and Henrietta listen to the radio. Sometime he drive me home in his car. He still live in the same little house. He been there so long, it look just like him. Two straight chairs always on the porch, turned against the wall. Porch railings with flower cans on them. He keep it painted now though.

Fresh and white. And guess what he collect just cause he like them? He collect shells. All kinds of shells. Terrapin, snail and all kinds of shells from the sea.

Matter of fact, that's how he got me up to the house again. He was telling Sofia bout some new shell he had that made a loud sea sound when you put it to your ear. Us went up to see it. It was big and heavy and speckled like a chicken and sure enough, seem like you could hear the waves or something crashing against your ear. None of us ever seen the ocean, but Mr —— learn about it from books. He order shells from books too, and they all over the place.

He don't say that much about them while you looking, but he hold each one like it just arrive.

Shug one time had a seashell, he say. Long time ago, when us first met. Big white thing look like a fan. She still love shells? he ast.

Naw, I say. She love elephants now.

He wait a little while, put all the shells back in place. Then he ast me, You like any special thing?

I love birds, I say.

You know, he say, you use to remind me of a bird. Way back when you first come to live with me. You was so skinny, Lord, he say. And the least little thing happen, you looked about to fly away.

You saw that, I say.

I saw it, he said, just too big a fool to let myself care.

Well, I say, us lived through it.

We still man and wife, you know, he say.

Naw, I say, we never was.

You know, he say, you look real good since you been up in Memphis.

Yeah, I say, Shug took good care of me.

How you make your living up there? he say.

Making pants, I say.

He say, I notice everybody in the family just about wearing pants you made. But you mean you turned it into a business?

That's right, I say. But I really started it right here in your house to keep from killing you.

He look down at the floor.

Shug help me make the first pair I ever did, I say. And then, like a fool, I start to cry.

He say, Celie, tell me the truth. You don't like me cause I'm a man?

I blow my nose. Take off they pants, I say, and men look like frogs to me. No matter how you kiss 'em, as far as I'm concern, frogs is what they stay.

I see, he say.

By the time I got back home I was feeling so bad I couldn't do nothing but sleep. I tried to work on some new pants I'm trying to make for pregnant women, but just the thought of anybody gitting pregnant make me want to cry.

Your sister,
Celie

Dear Nettie,

The only piece of mail Mr —— ever put directly in my hand is a telegram that come from the United States Department of Defense. It say the ship you and the children and your husband left Africa in was sunk by German mines off the coast of someplace call Gibralta. They think you all drowned. Plus, the same day, all the letters I wrote to you over the years come back unopen.

I sit here in this big house by myself trying to sew, but what good is sewing gon do? What good is anything? Being alive begin to seem like a awful strain.

Your sister,
Celie

Dearest Celie,

Tashi and her mother have run away. They have gone to join the *mbeles*. Samuel and the children and I were discussing it just yesterday, and we realized we do not even know for sure the *mbeles* exist. All we know is that they are said to live deep in the forest, that they welcome runaways, and that they harass the white man's plantations and plan his destruction – or at least for his removal from their continent.

Adam and Olivia are heartbroken because they love Tashi and miss her, and because no one who has gone to join the *mbeles* ever returned. We try to keep them busy around the compound and because there is so much sickness from malaria this season there is plenty for them to do. In plowing under the Olinka's yam crop and substituting canned and powdered goods, the planters destroyed what makes them resistant to malaria. Of course they did not know this, they only wanted to take the land for rubber, but the Olinka have been eating yams to prevent malaria and to control chronic blood disease for thousands and thousands of years. Left without a sufficient supply of yams, the people – what's left of them – are sickening and dying at an alarming rate.

To tell you the truth, I fear for our own health, and especially for the children. But Samuel feels we will probably be all right, having had bouts with malaria during the first years we were here.

And how are you, dearest sister? Nearly thirty years have passed without a word between us. For all I know you may be dead. As the time nears for us to come home, Adam and Olivia ask endless questions about you, few of which I can answer. Sometimes I tell them Tashi reminds me of you. And, because there is no one finer to them than Tashi, they glow with delight. But will you still have Tashi's honest and open spirit, I wonder, when we see you again? Or will years of childbearing and abuse from Mr —— have destroyed it? These are thoughts I don't pursue with the children, only with my beloved companion, Samuel, who advises me not to worry, to trust in God, and to have faith in the sturdiness of my sister's soul.

God is different to us now, after all these years in Africa. More spirit than ever before, and more internal. Most people think he has to look like something or someone – a roofleaf or Christ – but we don't. And not being tied to what God looks like, frees us.

When we return to America we must have long talks about this, Celie. And perhaps Samuel and I will found a new church in our community that has no idols in it whatsoever, in which each person's spirit is encouraged to seek God directly, his belief that this is possible strengthened by us as people who also believe.

There is little to do here for entertainment, as you can imagine. We read the papers and magazines from home, play any number of African games with the children. Rehearse the African children in parts of Shakespeare's plays – Adam was always very good as Hamlet giving his To Be or Not to Be soliloquy. Corrine had firm notions of what the children should be taught and saw to it that every good book advertised in the papers became part of their library. They know many things, and I think will not find American society such a shock, except for the hatred of black people, which is also very clear in all the news. But I worry about their very African independence of opinion and outspokenness, also their extreme self-centeredness. And we will be poor, Celie, and it will be years no doubt before we even own a home. How will they manage the hostility towards them, having grown up here? When I think of them in America I see them as much younger than they appear here. Much more naive. The worst we have had to endure here is indifference and a certain understandable shallowness in our personal relationships – excluding our relationship with Catherine and Tashi. After all, the Olinka know we can leave, they must stay. And, of course, none of this has to do with color, And –

Dearest Celie,

Last night I stopped writing because Olivia came in to tell me Adam is missing. He can only have gone after Tashi.

Pray for his safety,

Your sister, Nettie

Dearest Nettie,

Sometimes I think Shug never love me. I stand looking at my naked self in the looking glass. What would she love? I ast myself. My hair is short and kinky because I don't straighten it anymore. Once Shug say she love it no need to. My skin dark. My nose just a nose. My lips just lips. My body just any woman's body going through the changes of age. Nothing special here for nobody to love. No honey colored curly hair, no cuteness. Nothing young and fresh. My heart must be young and fresh though, it feel like it blooming blood.

I talk to myself a lot, standing in front the mirror. Celie, I say, happiness was just a trick in your case. Just cause you never had any before Shug, you thought it was time to have some, and that it was gon last. Even thought you had the trees with you. The whole earth. The stars. But look at you. When Shug left, happiness desert.

Every once in a while I git a postcard from Shug. Her and Germaine in New York, in California. Gone to see Mary Agnes and Grady in Panama.

Mr —— seem to be the only one understand my feeling.

I know you hate me for keeping you from Nettie, he say. And now she dead.

But I don't hate him, Nettie. And I don't believe you dead. How can you be dead if I still feel you? Maybe, like God, you changed into something different that I'll have to speak to in a different way, but you not dead to me Nettie. And never will be. Sometime when I git tired of talking to myself I talk to you. I even try to reach our children.

Mr —— still can't believe I have children. Where you git children from? he ast.

My stepdaddy, I say.

You mean he knowed he was the one damage you all along? he ast.

I say, Yeah.

Mr —— shake his head.

After all the evil he done I know you wonder why I don't hate him. I don't hate him for two reasons. One, he love Shug. And two, Shug use to love him. Plus, look like he trying to make something out himself. I don't mean just that he work and he clean up after himself and he appreciate some of the things God was playful enough to make. I mean when you talk to him now he really listen, and one time, out of nowhere in the conversation us was having, he said Celie, I'm satisfied this the first time I ever lived on Earth as a natural man. It feel like a new experience.

Sofia and Harpo always try to set me up with some man. They know I love Shug but they think womens love just by accident, anybody handy likely to do. Everytime I go to Harpo's some little policy salesman git all up in my face. Mr —— have to come to the rescue. He tell the man, This lady my wife. The man vanish out the door.

Us sit, have a cold drink. Talk about our days together with Shug. Talk about the time she come home sick. The little crooked song she use to sing. All our fine evenings down at Harpo's.

You was even sewing good way back then, he say. I remember the nice little dresses Shug always wear.

Yeah, I say. Shug could wear a dress.

Remember the night Sofia knock Mary Agnes' toofs out? he ast.

Who could forget it? I say.

Us don't say nothing bout Sofia's troubles. Us still can't laugh at that. Plus, Sofia still have trouble with that family. Well, trouble with Miss Eleanor Jane.

You just don't know, say Sofia, what that girl done put me through. You know how she use to bother me all the time when she had problems at home? Well finally she start bothering me when anything good happen. Soon as she snag that man she married she come running to me. Oh, Sofia, she say, you just have to meet Stanley Earl. And before I can say anything, Stanley Earl is in the middle of my front room.

How you, Sofia, he say, grinning and sticking out his hand. Miss Eleanor Jane done told me so much about you.

I wonder if she told him they made me sleep up under their house, say Sofia. But I don't ask. I try to be polite, act pleasant. Henrietta turn the radio up loud in the back room. I have to almost holler to make myself understood. They stand round looking at the children's pictures on the wall and saying how good my boys look in they army uniforms.

Where they fighting? Stanley Earl want to know.

They in the service right here in Georgia, I say. But pretty soon they be bound for overseas.

He ast me do I know which part they be station in? France, Germany or the Pacific.

I don't know where none of that is so I say, Naw. He say he want to fight but got to stay home and run his daddy's cotton gin.

Army got to wear clothes, he say, if they fighting in Europe. Too bad they not fighting in Africa. He laugh. Miss Eleanor Jane smile. Henrietta turn the dial high as it can go. Got on some real sorry whitefolks music sound like I don't know what. Stanley Earl snap his fingers and try to tap one of his good size foots. He got a long head go straight up and hair cut so short it look fuzzy. His eyes real bright blue and never hardly blink. Good God, I think.

Sofia raise me, practically, say Miss Eleanor Jane. Don't know what we would have done without her.

Well, say Stanley Earl, everybody round here raise by colored. That's how come we turn out so well. He wink at me, say, Well Sugar Pie, to Miss Eleanor Jane, time for us to mosey along.

She leap up like somebody stuck her with a pin. How Henrietta doing? she ast. Then she whisper, I brought her something with yams so well hid she won't never suspect. She run out to the car and come back with a tuna casserole.

Well, say Sofia, one thing you have to say for Miss Eleanor Jane, her dishes almost always fool Henrietta. And that mean a lots to me. Of course I never tell Henrietta where they come from. If I did, out the window they would go. Else she'd vomit, like it made her sick.

But finally, the end come to Sofia and Miss Eleanor Jane, I think. And it wasn't nothing to do with Henrietta, who hate Miss Eleanor Jane's guts. It was Miss Eleanor Jane herself and that baby she went and had. Every time Sofia turned round Miss Eleanor Jane was shoving Reynolds Stanley Earl in her face. He a little fat white something without much hair, look like he headed for the Navy.

Ain't little Reynolds sweet? say Miss Eleanor Jane, to Sofia. Daddy just love him, she say. Love having a grandchild name for him and look so much like him, too.

Sofia don't say nothing, stand there ironing some of Susie Q and Henrietta's clothes.

And so smart, say Eleanor Jane. Daddy say he never saw a smarter baby. Stanley Earl's mama say he smarter than Stanley Earl was when he was this age.

Sofia still don't say nothing.

Finally Eleanor Jane notice. And you know how some

whitefolks is, won't let well enough alone. If they want to bad enough, they gon harass a blessing from you if it kill.

Sofia mighty quiet this morning, Miss Eleanor Jane say, like she just talking to Reynolds Stanley. He stare back at her out of his big stuck open eyes.

Don't you think he sweet? she ast again.

He sure fat, say Sofia, turning over the dress she ironing.

And he sweet, too, say Miss Eleanor Jane.

Just as plump as he can be, say Sofia. And tall.

But he sweet, too, say Eleanor Jane. And he smart. She haul off and kiss him up side the head. He rub his head, say Yee.

Ain't he the smartest baby you ever saw? she ast Sofia.

He got a nice size head on him, say Sofia. You know some peoples place a lot of weight on head size. Not a whole lot of hair on it either. He gon be cool this summer, for sure. She fold the piece she iron and put it on a chair.

Just a sweet, smart, cute, *innocent* little baby boy, say Miss Eleanor Jane. Don't you just love him? she ast Sofia point blank. Sofia sigh. Put down her iron. Stare at Miss Eleanor Jane and Reynolds Stanley. All the time me and Henrietta over in the corner playing pitty pat. Henrietta act like Miss Eleanor Jane ain't alive, but both of us hear the way the iron sound when Sofia put it down. The sound have a lot of old and new stuff in it.

No ma'am, say Sofia. I do not love Reynolds Stanley Earl. Now. That's what you been trying to find out ever since he was born. And now you know.

Me and Henrietta look up. Miss Eleanor Jane just that quick done put Reynolds Stanley on the floor where he crawling round knocking stuff over. Head straight for Sofia's stack of ironed clothes and pull it down on his head. Sofia take up the clothes, straighten them out, stand by the ironing board with her hand on the iron. Sofia the kind of woman no matter what she have in her hand it look like a weapon.

Eleanor Jane start to cry. She always have felt something for Sofia. If not for her, Sofia never would have survive living in her daddy's house. But so what? Sofia never wanted to be there in the first place. Never wanted to leave her own children.

Too late to cry, Miss Eleanor Jane, say Sofia. All us can do now is laugh. Look at him, she say. And she do laugh. He can't even walk and already he in my house messing it up. Did I ast him to come? Do I care whether he sweet or not? Will it make any difference in the way he grow up to treat me what I think?

You just don't like him cause he look like daddy, say Miss Eleanor Jane.

You don't like him cause he look like daddy, say Sofia. I don't feel nothing about him at all. I don't love him, I don't hate him. I just wish he couldn't run loose all the time messing up folks stuff.

All the time! All the time! say Miss Eleanor Jane. Sofia, he just a baby. Not even a year old. He only been here five or six times.

I feel like he been here forever, say Sofia.

I just don't understand, say Miss Eleanor Jane. All the other colored women I know love children. The way you feel is something unnatural.

I love children, say Sofia. But all the colored women that say they love yours is lying. They don't love Reynolds Stanley any more than I do. But if you so badly raise as to ast 'em, what you expect them to say? Some colored people so scared of whitefolks they claim to love the cotton gin.

But he just a little baby! say Miss Eleanor Jane, like saying this is spose to clear up everything.

What you want from me? say Sofia. I feel something for you because out of all the people in your daddy's house you showed me some human kindness. But on the other hand, out of all the people in your daddy's house, I showed you some. Kind feeling is all I have to offer you. I don't have nothing to offer your relatives but just what they offer me. I don't have nothing to offer him.

Reynolds Stanley by this time is over on Henrietta pallet look like trying to rape her foot. Finally he start to chew her leg and Henrietta reach up on the windowsill and hand him a cracker.

I feel like you the only person love me, say Miss Eleanor Jane. Mama only love Junior, she say. Cause that's who daddy really love.

Well, say Sofia. You got your own husband to love you now.

Look like he don't love nothing but that cotton gin, she say. Ten o'clock at night and he still down there working. When he not working, he playing poker with the boys. My brother see a lot more of Stanley Earl than I do.

Maybe you ought to leave him, say Sofia. You got kin in Atlanta, go stay with some of them. Git a job.

Miss Eleanor Jane toss her hair back, act like she don't even hear this, it such a wild notion.

I got my own troubles, say Sofia, and when Reynolds Stanley grow up, he's gon be one of them.

But he won't, say Miss Eleanor Jane. I'm his mama and I won't let him be mean to colored.

You and whose army? say Sofia. The first word he likely to speak won't be nothing he learn from you.

You telling me I won't even be able to love my own son, say Miss Eleanor Jane.

No, say Sofia. That not what I'm telling you. I'm telling you I won't be able to love your own son. You can love him just as much as you want to. But be ready to suffer the consequences. That's how the colored live.

Little Reynolds Stanley all up on top Henrietta's face by

now, just slobbering and sucking. Trying to kiss. Any second I think she gon knock him silly. But she lay real still while he zamine her. Every once in a while he act like he peeking into her eyeball. Then he sit down with a bounce on top her chest and grin. He take one of her playing cards and try to give her a bite of it.

Sofia come over and lift him off.

He not bothering me, say Henrietta. He make me tickle.

He bother me, say Sofia.

Well, Miss Eleanor Jane say to the baby, picking him up, we not wanted here. She say it real sad, like she done run out of places to go.

Thank you for all you done for us, say Sofia. She don't look so good herself, and a little water stand in her eyes. After Miss Eleanor Jane and Reynolds Stanley leave, she say, It's times like this make me know us didn't make this world. And all the colored folks talking bout loving everybody just ain't looked hard at what they thought they said.

So what else new?

Well, your sister too crazy to kill herself. Most times I feels like shit but I felt like shit before in my life and what happen? I had me a fine sister name Nettie. I had me another fine woman friend name Shug. I had me some fine children growing up in Africa, singing and writing verses. The first two months was hell though, I tell the world. But now Shug's six months is come and gone and she ain't come back. And I try to teach my heart not to want nothing it can't have.

Besides, she give me so many good years. Plus, she learning new things in her new life. Now she and Germaine staying with one of her children.

Dear Celie, she wrote me, Me and Germaine ended up in Tucson, Arizona where one of my children live. The other two alive and turned out well but they didn't want to see me. Somebody told them I lives a evil life. This one say he want to see his mama no matter what. He live in a little mud looking house like they have out here, call adobe, so you know I feels right at home (smile). He a schoolteacher too and work on the Indian reservation. They call him the black white man. They have a word that mean that, too, and it really bother him. But even if he try to tell them how he feel, they don't seem to care. They so far gone nothing strangers say mean nothing. Everybody not a Indian they got no use for. I hate to see his feelings hurt, but that's life.

It was Germaine who had the idea to look up my children. He notice how I always love dressing him up and playing with his hair. He didn't make it like a mean suggestion. He just said if I knowed how my children was doing I would probably feel better in my life.

This son we staying with is name James. His wife is name Cora Mae. They have two kids name Davis and Cantrell. He say he thought something was funny bout his mama (my mama) cause she and big daddy was so old and strict and set in they ways. But still, he felt a lot of love from them, he say.

Yeah son, I tell him. They had a lot of love to give. But I needed love plus understanding. They run a little short of that.

They *been* dead now, he say. Nine or ten years. Sent us all to school as far as they could.

You know I never think bout mama and daddy. You know how tough I think I is. But now that they dead and I see my children doing well, I like to think about them. Maybe when I come back I can put some flowers on they graves.

Oh, she write me now near bout every week. Long newsy letters full of stuff she thought she had forgot. Plus stuff bout the desert and the Indians and the rocky mountains. I wish I could be traveling with her, but thank God she able to do it. Sometimes I feel mad at her. Feel like I could scratch her hair right off her head. But then I think, Shug got a right to live too. She got a right to look over the world in whatever company she choose. Just cause I love her don't take away none of her rights.

The only thing bother me is she don't never say nothing bout coming back. And I miss her. I miss her friendship so much that if she want to come back here dragging Germaine I'd make them both welcome, or die trying. Who am I to tell her who to love? My job just to love her good and true myself.

Mr —— ast me the other day what it is I love so much bout Shug. He say he love her style. He say to tell the truth, Shug act more manly than most men. I mean she upright, honest. Speak her mind and the devil take the hindmost, he say. You know Shug will fight, he say. Just like Sofia. She bound to live her life and be herself no matter what.

Mr —— think all this is stuff men do. But Harpo not like this, I tell him. You not like this. What Shug got is womanly it seem like to me. Specially since she and Sofia the ones got it.

Sofia and Shug not like men, he say, but they not like women either.

You mean they not like you or me.

They hold they own, he say. And it's different.

What I love best bout Shug is what she been through, I say. When you look in Shug's eyes you know she been where she been, seen what she seen, did what she did. And now she know.

That's the truth, say Mr ——.

And if you don't git out the way, she'll tell you about it.

Amen, he say. Then he say something that really surprise me cause it so thoughtful and common sense. When it come to what folks do together with they bodies, he say, anybody's guess is as good as mine. But when you talk bout love I don't have to guess. I have love and I have been love. And I thank

God he let me gain understanding enough to know love can't be halted just cause some peoples moan and groan. It don't surprise me you love Shug Avery, he say. I have love Shug Avery all my life.

What load of bricks fell on you? I ast.

No bricks, he say. Just experience. You know, everybody bound to git some of that sooner or later. All they have to do is stay alive. And I start to git mine real heavy long about the time I told Shug it was true that I beat you cause you was you and not her.

I told her, I say.

I know it, he say, and I don't blame you. If a mule could tell folks how it's treated, it would. But you know some womens would have just love to hear they man say he beat his wife cause she wasn't them. Shug one time was like that bout Annie Julia. Both of us messed over my first wife a scandless. And she never told nobody. Plus, she didn't have nobody to tell. After they married her off to me her folks behave like they'd throwed her down a well. Or off the face of the earth. I didn't want her. I wanted Shug. But my daddy was the boss. He give me the wife he wanted me to have.

But Shug spoke right up for you, Celie, he say. She say Albert, you been mistreating somebody I love. So as far as you concern, I'm gone. I couldn't believe it, he say. All along in there we was as hot for each other as two pistols. Excuse me, he say. But we was. I tried to laugh it off. But she meant what she said.

I tried to tease her. You don't love old dumb Celie, I said. She ugly and skinny and can't hold a candle to you. She can't even screw.

What I want to say that for. From what she tell me, Shug said, she don't have no reason to screw. You on and off like a jackrabbit. Plus, she say, Celie say you not always clean. And she turn up her nose.

I wanted to kill you, said Mr —— and I did slap you around a couple of times. I never understood how you and Shug got along so well together and it bothered the hell out of me. When she was mean and nasty to you, I understood. But when I looked around and the two of you was always doing each other's hair, I start to worry.

She still feel for you, I say.

Yeah, he say. She feel like I'm her brother.

What so bad about that, I ast. Don't her brothers love her?

Them clowns, he say. They still act the fool I use to be.

Well, I say, we all have to start somewhere if us want to do better, and our own self is what us have to hand.

I'm real sorry she left you, Celie. I remember how I felt when she left me.

Then the old devil put his arms around me and just stood there on the porch with me real quiet. Way after while I bent my stiff neck onto his shoulder. Here us is, I thought, two old fools left over from love, keeping each other company under the stars.

Other times he want to know bout my children.

I told him you say they both wear long robes, sort of like dresses. That was the day he come to visit me while I was sewing and ast me what was so special bout my pants.

Anybody can wear them, I said.

Men and women not suppose to wear the same thing, he said. Men spose to wear the pants.

So I said, You ought to tell that to the mens in Africa.

Say what? he ast. First time he ever thought bout what Africans do.

People in Africa try to wear what feel comfortable in the heat, I say. Of course, missionaries have they own ideas bout dress. But left to themself, Africans wear a little sometimes, or a lot, according to Nettie. But men and women both preshate a nice dress.

Robe you said before, he say.

Robe, dress. Not pants, anyhow.

Well, he say. I'll be dog.

And men sew in Africa, too, I say.

They do? he ast.

Yeah, I say. They not so backward as mens here.

When I was growing up, he said, I use to try to sew along with mama cause that's what she was always doing. But everybody laughed at me. But you know, I liked it.

Well, nobody gon laugh at you now, I said. Here, help me stitch in these pockets.

But I don't know how, he say.

I'll show you, I said. And I did.

Now us sit sewing and talking and smoking our pipes.

Guess what, I say to him, folks in Africa where Nettie and the children is believe white people is black peoples children.

Naw, he say, like this interesting but his mind really on the slant of his next stitch.

They named Adam some other name soon as he arrive. They say the white missionaries before Nettie and them come told them all about Adam from the white folks point of view and what the white folks know. But they know who Adam is from they own point of view. And for a whole lot longer time ago.

And who that? Mr ——— ast.

The first man that was white. Not the first man. They say nobody so crazy they think they can say who was the first man. But everybody notice the first white man cause he was white.

Mr ——— frown, look at the different color thread us got. Thread his needle, lick his finger, tie a knot.

They say everybody before Adam was black. Then one day some woman they just right away kill, come out with this colorless baby. They thought at first it was something she ate.

But then another one had one and also the women start to have twins. So the people start to put the white babies and the twins to death. So really Adam wasn't even the first white man. He was just the first one the people didn't kill.

Mr —— look at me real thoughtful. He not such a bad looking man, you know, when you come right down to it. And now it do begin to look like he got a lot of feeling hind his face.

Well, I say, you know black folks have what you call albinos to this day. But you never hear of white folks having nothing black unless some black man been messing with 'em. And no white folks been in Africa back yonder when all this happen.

So these Olinka people heard about Adam and Eve from the white missionaries and they heard about how the serpent tricked Eve and how God chased them out of the garden of Eden. And they was real curious to hear this, cause after they had chased the white Olinka children out of the village they hadn't hardly thought no more about it. Nettie say one thing about Africans, Out of sight, out of mind. And another thing, they don't like nothing around them that look or act different. They want everybody to be just alike. So you know somebody white wouldn't last long. She say seem like to her the Africans throwed out the white Olinka peoples for how they look. They throwed out the rest of us, all us who become slaves, for how us act. Seem like us just wouldn't do right no matter how us try. Well, you know how niggers is. Can't nobody tell 'em nothing even today. Can't be rule. Every nigger you see got a kingdom in his head.

But guess what else, I say to Mr ——. When the missionaries got to the part bout Adam and Eve being naked, the Olinka peoples nearly bust out laughing. Especially when the missionaries tried to make them put on clothes because of this. They tried to explain to the missionaries that it was *they* who put Adam and Eve out of the village because they *was* naked. Their word for naked is white. But since they are covered by color they are not naked. They said anybody looking at a white person can tell they naked, but black people can not be naked because they can not be white.

Yeah, say Mr ———. But they was wrong.

Right, I said. Adam and Eve prove it. What they did, these Olinka peoples, was throw out they own children, just cause they was a little different.

I bet they do that same kind of stuff today, Mr ——— say.

Oh, from what Nettie say, them Africans is a mess. And you know what the bible say, the fruit don't fall too far from the tree. And something else, I say. Guess who they say the snake is?

Us, no doubt, say Mr ———.

Right, I say. Whitefolks sign for they parents. They was so mad to git throwed out and told they was naked they made up they minds to crush us wherever they find us, same as they would a snake.

You reckon? Mr ——— ast.

That's what these Olinka peoples say. But they say just like they know history before the white children start to come, they know the future after the biggest of 'em leave. They say they know these particular children and they gon kill each other off, they still so mad bout being unwanted. Gon kill off a lot of other folk too who got some color. In fact, they gon kill off so much of the earth and the colored that everybody gon hate them just like they hate us today. Then they will become the new serpent. And wherever a white person is found he'll be crush by somebody not white, just like they do us today. And some of the Olinka peoples believe life will just go on and on like this forever. And every million years or so something will happen to the earth and folks will change the way they look. Folks might start growing two heads one of these days, for all us know, and then the folks with one head will send 'em all someplace else. But some of 'em don't think like this. They think, after the biggest of the white folks no longer on the earth, the only way to stop making somebody the serpent is for everybody to accept everybody else as a child of God, or one mother's children, no matter what they look like or how they act. And guess what else about the snake?

What? he ast.

These Olinka peoples worship it. They say who knows, maybe it is kinfolks, but for sure it's the smartest, cleanest, slickest thing they ever seen.

These folks sure must have a heap of time just to sit and think, say Mr ———.

Nettie say they real good at thinking, I say. But they think so much in terms of thousands of years they have a hard time gitting themself through one.

So what they name Adam?

Something sound like Omatangu, I say. It mean a un-naked man somewhere near the first one God made that knowed what he was. A whole lot of the men that come before the first man was men, but none of 'em didn't know it. You know how long it take some mens to notice anything, I say.

Took me long enough to notice you such good company, he say. And he laugh.

He ain't Shug, but he begin to be somebody I can talk to.

And no matter how much the telegram said you must be drown, I still git letters from you.

Your sister,
Celie

Dear Celie,

After two and a half months Adam and Tashi returned! Adam overtook Tashi and her mother and some other members of our compound as they were nearing the village where the white woman missionary had lived, but Tashi would not hear of turning back, nor would Catherine, and so Adam accompanied them to the *mbeles* encampment.

Oh, he says, it is the most extraordinary place!

You know, Celie, in Africa there is a huge depression in the earth called the great rift valley, but it is on the other side of the continent from where we are. However, according to Adam, there is a 'small' rift on our side, several thousand acres large and even deeper than the great rift, which covers millions of acres. It is a place set so deep into the earth that it can only really be seen, Adam thinks, from the air, and then it would seem just an overgrown canyon. Well, in this overgrown canyon are a thousand people from dozens of African tribes, and even one colored man – Adam swears – from Alabama! There are farms. There is a school. An infirmary. A temple. And there are male and female warriors who do indeed go on missions of sabotage against the white plantations.

But all this seemed more a marvel in the recounting than in the actual experiencing of it, if I am any judge of Adam and Tashi. Their minds seem to have been completely riveted on each other.

I wish you could have seen them as they staggered into the

compound. Filthy as hogs, hair as wild as could be. Sleepy. Exhausted. Smelly. God knows. But still arguing.

Just because I came back with you, don't think I am saying yes to marriage, says Tashi.

Oh yes you are, says Adam, heatedly, but through a yawn. You promised your mother. I promised your mother.

Nobody in America will like me, says Tashi.

I will like you, says Adam.

Olivia ran and enfolded Tashi in her arms. Ran about preparing food and a bath.

Last night, after Tashi and Adam had slept most of the day, we had a family conference. We informed them that because so many of our people had gone to join the *mbeles* and the planters were beginning to bring in Moslem workers from the North, and because it was time for us to do so, we would be leaving for home in a matter of weeks.

Adam announced his desire to marry Tashi.

Tashi announced her refusal to be married.

And then, in that honest, forthright way of hers, she gave her reasons. Paramount among them that, because of the scarification marks on her cheeks Americans would look down on her as a savage and shun her, and whatever children she and Adam might have. That she had seen the magazines we receive from home and that it was very clear to her that black people did not truly admire blackskinned black people like herself, and especially did not admire blackskinned black women. They bleach their faces, she said. They fry their hair. They try to look naked.

Also, she continued, I fear Adam will be distracted by one of these naked looking women and desert me. Then I would have no country, no people, no mother and no husband and brother.

You'd have a sister, said Olivia.

Then Adam spoke. He asked Tashi to forgive his initial stupid response to the scarification. And to forgive the repugnance he'd felt about the female initiation ceremony. He assured Tashi that it was she he loved and that in America she would have country, people, parents, sister, husband, brother and lover, and that whatever befell her in America would also be his own choice and his own lot.

Oh, Celie.

So, the next day, our boy came to us with scars identical to Tashi's on his cheeks.

And they are so happy. So happy, Celie. Tashi and Adam Omatangu.

Samuel married them, of course, and all the people left in the compound came to wish them happiness and an abundance of roofleaf forever. Olivia stood up with the bride and a friend of Adam's — a man too old to have joined the *mbeles* — stood up with him. Immediately after the wedding we left the compound, riding in a lorry that took us to a boat at the coast inlet that flows out to sea.

In a few weeks, we will all be home.

Your loving sister,
Nettie

Dear Nettie,

Mr —— talk to Shug a lot lately by telephone. He say as soon as he told her my sister and her family was missing, she and Germaine made a beeline for the State department trying to find out what happen. He say Shug say it just kill her to think I'm down here suffering from not knowing. But nothing happen at the State department. Nothing at the department of defense. It's a big war. So much going on. One ship lost feel like nothing, I guess. Plus, colored don't count to those people.

Well, they just don't know, and never did. Never will. And so what? I know you on your way home and you may not git here till I'm ninety, but one of these days I do expect to see your face.

Meanwhile, I hired Sofia to clerk in our store. Kept the white man Alphonso got to run it, but put Sofia in there to wait on colored cause they never had nobody in a store to wait on 'em before and nobody in a store to treat 'em nice. Sofia real good at selling stuff too cause she act like she don't care if you buy or not. No skin off her nose. And then if you do decide to buy anyhow, well, she might exchange a few pleasant words with you. Plus, she scare that white man. Anybody else colored he try to call 'em auntie or something. First time he try that with Sofia she ast him which colored man his mama sister marry.

I ast Harpo do he mind if Sofia work.

What I'm gon mind for? he say. It seem to make her happy. And I can take care of anything come up at home.

Anyhow, he say, Sofia got me a little help for when Henrietta need anything special to eat or git sick.

Yeah, say Sofia. Miss Eleanor Jane gon look in on Henrietta and every other day promise to cook her something she'll eat. You know white people have a look of machinery in they kitchen. She whip up stuff with yams you'd never believe. Last week she went and made yam ice cream.

How this happen? I ast. I thought the two of you was through.

Oh, say Sofia. It finally dawn on her to ast her mama why I come to work for them.

I don't expect it to last, though, say Harpo. You know how they is.

Do her peoples know? I ast.

They know, say Sofia. They carrying on just like you know they would. Whoever heard of a white woman working for niggers, they rave. She tell them, Whoever heard of somebody like Sofia working for trash.

She bring Reynolds Stanley with her? I ast.

Henrietta say she don't mind him.

Well, say Harpo, I'm satisfied if her menfolks against her helping you, she gon quit.

Let her quit, say Sofia. It not my salvation she working for. And if she don't learn she got to face judgment for herself, she won't even have live.

Well, you got me behind you, anyway, say Harpo. And I loves every judgment you ever made. He move up and kiss her where her nose was stitch.

Sofia toss her head. Everybody learn something in life, she say. And they laugh.

Speaking of learning. Mr —— say one day us was sewing out on the porch, I first start to learn all them days ago I use to sit up there on my porch, staring out cross the railing.

Just miserable. That's what I was. And I couldn't understand why us have life at all if all it can do most times is make us feel bad. All I ever wanted in life was Shug Avery, he say. And one while, all she wanted in life was me. Well, us couldn't have each other, he say. I got Annie Julia. Then you. All them rotten children. She got Grady and who know who all. But still, look like she come out better than me. A lot of people love Shug, but nobody but Shug love me.

Hard not to love Shug, I say. She know how to love somebody back.

I tried to do something bout my children after you left me. But by that time it was too late. Bub come with me for two weeks, stole all my money, laid up on the porch drunk. My girls so far off into mens and religion they can't hardly talk. Everytime they open they mouth some kind of plea come out. Near bout to broke my sorry heart.

If you know your heart sorry, I say, that mean it not quite as spoilt as you think.

Anyhow, he say, you know how it is. You ast yourself one question, it lead to fifteen. I start to wonder why us need love. Why us suffer. Why us black. Why us men and women. Where do children really come from. It didn't take long to realize I didn't hardly know nothing. And that if you ast yourself why you black or a man or a woman or a bush it don't mean nothing if you don't ast why you here, period.

So what you think? I ast.

I think us here to wonder, myself. To wonder. To ast. And that in wondering bout the big things and asting bout the big things, you learn about the little ones, almost by accident. But you never know nothing more about the big things than you start out with. The more I wonder, he say, the more I love.

And people start to love you back, I bet, I say.

They do, he say, surprise. Harpo seem to love me. Sofia

and the children. I think even ole evil Henrietta love me a little bit, but that's cause she know she just as big a mystery to me as the man in the moon.

Mr —— is busy patterning a shirt for folks to wear with my pants.

Got to have pockets, he say. Got to have loose sleeves. And definitely you not spose to wear it with no tie. Folks wearing ties look like they being lynch.

And then, just when I know I can live content without Shug, just when Mr —— done ast me to marry him again, this time in the spirit as well as in the flesh, and just after I say Naw, I still don't like frogs, but let's us be friends, Shug write me she coming home.

Now. Is this life or not?

I be so calm.

If she come, I be happy. If she don't, I be content.

And then I figure this the lesson I was suppose to learn.

Oh Celie, she say, stepping out of the car, dress like a moving star, I missed you more than I missed my own mama.

Us hug.

Come on in, I say.

Oh, the house look so nice, she say, when us git to her room. You know I love pink.

Got you some elephants and turtles coming, too, I say.

Where your room? she ast.

Down the hall, I say.

Let's go see it, she say.

Well, here it is, I say, standing in the door. Everything in my room purple and red cept the floor, that painted bright yellow. She go right to the little purple frog perch on my mantlepiece.

What this? she ast.

Oh, I say, a little something Albert carve for me.

She look at me funny for a minute, I look at her. Then us laugh.

Where Germaine at? I ast.

In college, she say. Wilberforce. Can't let all that talent go to waste. Us through, though, she say. He feel just like family now. Like a son. Maybe a grandson. What you and Albert been up to? she ast.

Nothing much, I say.

She say, I know Albert and I bet he been up to *something*, with you looking as fine as you look.

Us sew, I say. Make idle conversation.

How idle? she ast.

What do you know, I think. Shug jealous. I have a good mind to make up a story just to make her feel bad. But I don't.

Us talk bout you, I say. How much us love you.

She smile, come put her head on my breast. Let out a long breath.

Your sister,
Celie

Dear God. Dear stars, dear trees, dear sky, dear peoples. Dear
Everything. Dear God.

Thank you for bringing my sister Nettie and our children
home.

Wonder who that coming yonder? ast Albert, looking up
the road. Us can see the dust just aflying.

Me and him and Shug sitting out on the porch after dinner.
Talking. Not talking. Rocking and fanning flies. Shug mention
she don't want to sing in public no more – well, maybe a
night or two at Harpo's. Think maybe she retire. Albert say
he want her to try on his new shirt. I talk bout Henrietta.
Sofia. My garden and the store. How things doing generally.
So much in the habit of sewing something I stitch up a bunch
of scraps, try to see what I can make. The weather cool for
the last of June, and sitting on the porch with Albert and
Shug feel real pleasant. Next week be the fourth of July and
us plan a big family reunion outdoors here at my house. Just
hope the cool weather hold.

Could be the mailman, I say. Cept he driving a little fast.

Could be Sofia, say Shug. You know she drive like a maniac.

Could be Harpo, say Albert. But it not.

By now the car stop under the trees in the yard and all
these peoples dress like old folks git out.

A big tall whitehaired man with a backward turn white
collar, a little dumpty woman with her gray hair in plaits cross
on top her head. A tall youngish man and two robust looking
youngish women. The whitehaired man say something to the

driver of the car and the car leave. They all stand down there at the edge of the drive surrounded by boxes and bags and all kinds of stuff.

By now my heart is in my mouth and I can't move.

It's Nettie, Albert say, gitting up.

All the people down by the drive look up at us. They look at the house. The yard. Shug and Albert's cars. They look round at the fields. Then they commence to walk real slow up the walk to the house.

I'm so scared I don't know what to do. Feel like my mind stuck. I try to speak, nothing come. Try to git up, almost fall. Shug reach down and give me a helping hand. Albert press me on the arm.

When Nettie's foot come down on the porch I almost die. I stand swaying, tween Albert and Shug. Nettie stand swaying tween Samuel and I reckon it must be Adam. Then us both start to moan and cry. Us totter toward one nother like us use to do when us was babies. Then us feel so weak when us touch, us knock each other down. But what us care? Us sit and lay there on the porch inside each other's arms.

After while, she say *Celie*.

I say *Nettie*.

Little bit more time pass. Us look round at a lot of peoples knees. Nettie never let go my waist. This my husband Samuel, she say, pointing up. These our children Olivia and Adam and this Adam's wife Tashi, she say.

I point up at my peoples. This Shug and Albert, I say.

Everybody say Pleased to Meetcha. Then Shug and Albert start to hug everybody one after the other.

Me and Nettie finally git up off the porch and I hug my children. And I hug Tashi. Then I hug Samuel.

Why us always have family reunion on July 4th, say Henrietta, mouth poke out, full of complaint. It so hot.

White people busy celebrating they independence from England July 4th, say Harpo, so most black folks don't have to work. Us can spend the day celebrating each other.

Ah, Harpo, say Mary Agnes, sipping some lemonade, I didn't know you knowed history. She and Sofia working together on the potato salad. Mary Agnes come back home to pick up Suzie Q. She done left Grady, move back to Memphis and live with her sister and her ma. They gon look after Suzie Q while she work. She got a lot of new songs, she say, and not too knocked out to sing 'em.

After while, being with Grady, I couldn't think, she say. Plus, he not a good influence for no child. Course, I wasn't either, she say. Smoking so much reefer.

Everybody make a lot of miration over Tashi. People look at her and Adam's scars like that's they business. Say they never suspect African ladies could look so *good*. They make a fine couple. Speak a little funny, but us gitting use to it.

What your people love best to eat over there in Africa? us ast.

She sort of blush and say *barbecue*.

Everybody laugh and stuff her with one more piece.

I feel a little peculiar round the children. For one thing, they grown. And I see they think me and Nettie and Shug and Albert and Samuel and Harpo and Sofia and Jack and Odessa real old and don't know much what going on. But I don't think us feel old at all. And us so happy. Matter of fact, I think this the youngest us ever felt.

Amen

I thank everybody in this book for coming.
A.W., author and medium